JOHN GILL

LITTLE, BROWN AND COMPANY
BOSTON   TORONTO

FIRST EDITION

LIBRARY OF CONGRESS CATALOGING IN PUBLICATION DATA

Gill, John.
  Kiki.

  I. Title.
PZ4.G474ki 1979 [PR6057.I55]   823'.9'14   79-10404
ISBN 0-316-31341-6

BP
Designed by Susan Windheim

PRINTED IN THE UNITED STATES OF AMERICA

Lady Gregory-Montfort, O.B.E.
c/o Hôtel Victoria Regina,
Promenade des Anglais,
Nice.

Dear Bea,
Alas, they've closed the American hospital at Villefranche now, and the pavement café further down
Boulevard Carnot where we drank our *pastis* is a
souvenir shop. Claudine, they say, has gone back to her
lover in the hills.

But in this story I have kept it the way it was and only
changed the character of things where necessary. And
of course you still live on, with your army of ghosts
(who else danced in the surf with Scott Fitzgerald or
exchanged such epigrams with Maugham?) and here I
give you another more recent one to add to them. He is
Ellis G. Sargesson, M.D., F.A.C.P., sometime physician
of the hospital of the University of Pennsylvania and of
the American hospital at Villefranche.

Maybe it will help to while away a few of those bleak
days when the mistral keeps you to your rooms, but I
warn you that you may not skip what you have always
called the *sexuel garni;* in this case it is essential to the
dish.

> *Amitiés,* from your friend
> JOHN

La Raze
Domme,
France

PART I

1

HE SHOULD NEVER HAVE TAKEN THE CARTONS UP TO HIS office at the hospital in the first place.

It had been his own stupid mistake, forgetting about the car being at the body shop. Now, leaving for home, he held them awkwardly while he fiddled with his key case trying to close the double lock of his door. In the end he had to stack them while he did it. He put the key case back in his fob pocket. He was a man for whom everything had a place. As he loaded himself with the cartons again, somewhere to the west, out in the Bay of Angels, he heard the first thunderclap of the approaching storm.

Then footsteps sounded around the corner of the corridor. He waited. All he wanted was out. And no fuss.

The footsteps died with the closing of the door. Sargesson moved off in the opposite direction, ignoring the usual way down to the main exit. Instead he made for the rear of the building. He could use the casualty elevator, which in any case gave easier access to the parking lot.

He walked carefully, without haste, along corridors whose long nineteenth-century windows looked down through the pale branches of the plane trees to the Villefranche roads. Cap Ferrat beyond looked as gray as a steel engraving. He passed the entrance to the Dispensary without turning his head and swung right into another shorter passage. Ahead of him the elevator shaft was empty behind the diamond trellis gates. He pressed the button and heard the faint hum of the motor begin. As it sank to eye level from the Pathology floor above, he saw with relief that it was empty. He opened the gates and stepped in. Reaching awkwardly for the control button, he stopped. Someone had called his name. Against the glare of a west window at the end of the passage, he couldn't see who it was. After a moment a gurney resolved itself and then the hunched figure of Le Chêne in a white jacket. Le Chêne rolled the gurney in beside Sargesson and, without checking, put out his hands for the cartons.

"No, it's okay. They're nothing. . . ." But Le Chêne took them from him as firmly as a nanny taking toys from a child at bedtime.

In a sense Le Chêne had a nanny's authority. He was the oldest of the orderlies and had been around ever since the place had belonged to the British and was called the Queen Victoria Memorial Hospital. He stood there watching Sargesson as the cage sank to the courtyard below. Sargesson knew it was hopeless to try to reclaim the cartons now and that Le Chêne would insist on loading them into the car. As he walked down the ramp from the elevator, his edgy mind raced off into the nightmare possibility of an accident, of an ambulance driving wildly through the gates and smashing into the gurney. The cartons would be flung down and split open, their contents scattered. The wall of sickening silence would form around him gradually as people gathered.

But when they walked down the ramp from the elevator through the close, storm-laden evening, the courtyard was empty. And as he paced beside the gurney the nightmare was replaced by a memory. It was only about eight months since he had walked like this behind Marion's coffin as the undertaker's men pushed it through seemingly endless rows of headstones to its final place in the cemetery at Caucade. One of the bearers, he remembered now, had smelt heavily of *anis,* a prophylactic, maybe, against his daily contact with the dead.

They reached his Peugeot, and again with the authority of the nursery Le Chêne took the keys from his hand and opened the trunk. He placed the cartons inside and seemed to spend hours moving them around until they were settled to his satisfaction.

"*Voilà,*" he said finally, and slammed down the lid.

The locking of the trunk released Sargesson at last from his stricture of embarrassment. After he'd thanked Le Chêne he even walked a little way back with him toward the block. "How is Thérèse?"

"Pains in the ass, as always, Docteur. All that sitting around . . ."

"We still miss her in the kitchen." For fifteen years Thérèse had cooked for the staff. "The food has never been so good since she left. Do tell her that we miss her."

He drove down to the cliff road and turned left toward Villefranche.

He drove mechanically, stopping and starting with the traffic stream as he had done for nearly a hundred evenings. For it was almost three months since he had moved into the new house. There had been alterations to be made, of course, though fewer in the end than he had expected, thanks in part to the Bellegarde Viaduct, which was nearby, and also in part to the British Air Force, which had tried to bomb it during World War II.

At Beaulieu he turned left and drove up to the Place Charles de Gaulle. Although the *halles* had closed, there were still a couple of stalls open in the street market. He parked the car, walked around to make sure the trunk was locked, and then crossed to the left-hand side of the market. From habit he always came here on Friday evenings, just as he shopped at the *halles* on Tuesday mornings and at other markets at Nice and Monte Carlo in between. It was only a small detail, but he didn't want to buy regularly at the same place. For that reason he had given up shopping in Villefranche. He didn't want *anyone* to know what he bought.

Today he stopped only twice, to buy a small partridge already plucked, and a quart of milk. He waited while they drew the partridge for him. On the way back to the car he stopped at a small market and bought a tin of artichoke hearts and another quart of milk. Waiting to pay, the short queue was imprisoned in a mirror above the checkout, like figures in some classical frieze, and he was momentarily surprised by his own reflection—stooped, ectomorphic, among a row of plump women. Except for his coloring, which was gray-blond, he was looking as usual just like a tintype of Abraham Lincoln. Unconsciously he drew a hand down his clawed cheeks as if he might smooth them out. He moved up to pay, transferring the plastic milk container carefully to the top of his basket.

He was halfway back to the car when someone behind him spoke his name quite clearly. "Dr. Sargesson?"

He turned, maybe too quickly. He said, "Oh . . . hello there." Looking down at her uncertainly, he tried to remember her name and whether she'd been a patient at the hospital, or whether she belonged to the distant social calendar of his life with Marion.

"Hilary Osgood," she said brightly. She moistened her lips each time she finished speaking as if conversation dried her up. "You treated my husband at the hospital."

Osgood, he thought, mentally turned over medical cards. "Did he have hemorrhoids?"

She laughed wildly. "Well, yes . . ." Her tongue came farther out than ever and a dull flush spread upward from her neck.

At that moment a huge trailer truck came crawling

by with a load of steel rods. She spoke rapidly and licked her lips again, but the words were lost and he shrugged his shoulders at the hopelessness of it. The driver slowed down, the truck crawled, the longueur of embarrassment seemed endlessly prolonged.

Waiting, she stared down at his basket and, his gaze following her own, saw the two containers of milk lying on the top.

Bugger the goddam milk, he thought. Before he could stop himself he was shouting, "Always make my yoghurt over the weekend."

Hilary Osgood opened her hands against the fading roar of the diesel. "What did you say?"

He repeated it fatuously. "Yoghurt-making day."

"Oh . . . sure." Her obvious bewilderment compounded the awkwardness still further.

He started to move away past her. "Must get along, Mrs. Osgood. Hope your husband is still in good shape."

"Oh yes . . . he's fine."

He walked quickly back to the car and harangued himself all the way. What a foul-up! The stupid bitch had probably not even *noticed* the milk and he had made the classic response of a man in panic and had started to *explain*. He got into the car and put the groceries on the seat beside him and waited there quietly before starting to drive.

It was okay, he decided finally as he searched for a rationale. It was okay. The alarm had been all in his mind. And even if it hadn't been and some of it had shown, it didn't matter all that much. Since Marion had died everyone knew he had succumbed to the eccentricities of a hermit.

He waited another minute. Waiting, he thought wryly, for insanity to return.

HE DROVE UP TO THE MIDDLE CORNICHE, AWAY FROM THE
storm that was piling up behind him.

Bellegarde was just beyond Eze, between the middle
and lower Corniche, and it was to there that he had
moved after Marion died. He had looked at over fifty
houses along the coast and the search had taken nearly
three months.

The day he found the house he'd left the car at
Villefranche station and taken the regional *métro* out to
Bellegarde-Plage. It was a day in early June with a little
high cloud coming in from the sea. He had concentrated on the area to the east of Nice because it was the
part most accessible to the hospital. He had made the
same journey to the Monaco area several times already,
though he had not seen this particular real estate agent

before, and he felt neither hopeful nor pessimistic. If he ever thought of himself objectively it was to realize that his work should not allow him hope or any other feeling that wasn't rooted in demonstrable fact. It was a negative essential in the same way that a lack of sensitivity was essential to a journalist.

Of the fifty-odd houses he had seen so far, only two at most had come anywhere near to having the kind of privacy he had specified. And there were other amenities, too, which were quintessential to his needs but which couldn't really be defined to a real estate agent without the embarrassment of long explanations.

There was no one to meet him when he left the entrance to the platform, so he walked idly along the street beyond. He was strolling back again when he saw the Citroën Ami. There was a real estate dealer's sticker on the rear window, and M. Chartier, when he left it, seemed to recognize Sargesson immediately.

They shook hands and Chartier gripped Sargesson's elbow solicitously. His brown intuitive eyes looked steadily into Sargesson's own; it was like the opening lesson from some course in sales sincerity. He held the passenger door while settling Sargesson into the car, all the time explaining that the Simca Maserati was being serviced that day. The Citroën heaved and sank under Sargesson's weight, making him feel as though he were mounting a live animal.

Chartier slipped the safety belt and took a cigarette from the console between them.

"A cigarette? They are American."

"I don't smoke."

"I only smoke rarely myself." The ashtray beside him was full but he dismissed it with a wave of his hand. "A terrible car . . . ," he said.

His black mustache was the same density as his eyebrows and all three moved constantly, making hieroglyphics of his conversation. Now, from the heights of rueful exasperation, they straightened out into lines of integrity. "Docteur, I think—I am almost positive—that I have the house for which you are looking. A Marquise once lived there." Marquises must have been thick on the coast because about half the houses Sargesson had seen had at some time belonged to one.

"That's great." He moved with what he hoped was visible impatience. "I don't have too much time. . . ."

But Chartier's plump hand was tilting this way and that between them. "The house I'm going to show you is very, very discreet. For *le weekend* . . ."

"It's not only for the weekends," Sargesson said sharply. "I hope to be there all the time except when I'm on duty."

"It is even better, then. You have excellent rail access here and three Corniches when you drive."

Chartier started the engine at last, but a stream of traffic was now passing.

They waited with the indicator flashing. "It is very secluded," he said, returning to the previous theme. "But the garden requires much work. There are trees growing right up to the house."

There was a slight gap coming in the traffic and

Sargesson found himself willing Chartier to take it. "Now," he said sharply. "Now!" But Chartier's timing was late and again they waited impotently.

They drove away up the hill at last and shortly afterward a turn in the road opened up a vista of blue sea. Through the arches of the enormous viaduct they had just left, the houses of Bellegarde-Plage were visible among a scattering of cypress and olive trees. They rocked on up through streets of Italianate villas dripping with plumbago and wisteria into the old town. The medieval buildings had been modernized by tradesmen and the pavements were cluttered with grass cutters and garden furniture and all the other impedimenta of out-of-town life. They crossed a center square with police vans parked outside the Gendarmerie and a huge statue of a *poilu* contemplating the helmet in his hand. Turning right, the old houses continued up the hill and Sargesson saw the brass plates of Paris bankers and insurance companies.

Above, they entered a newer area of the town spread out on the south face of a small hill. The richer bourgeoisie lived here in tall houses built of traditional white sandstone. Roofs of orange tiles bristled with dormer windows, and there were chic British cars like Jaguars and Rovers parked in the driveways. Sargesson feared another wild-goose chase.

As he moved uneasily, M. Chartier must have felt the shift in suspension, for he lifted his hand in a gesture of patience. *"Attendez,"* he said.

Shortly afterward they turned into a cul-de-sac with

only half a dozen smaller houses on either side. There was a screen of woodland at the end of it, and they parked on the grass where it began. Through the trees Sargesson could just see the hips and gables of an older house. Whatever gate had once been there was missing from its hinges and they walked up a driveway overgrown from disuse. Brambles pulled at his trouser legs and it was suddenly cold in the shadow of the trees. The drift of air was just strong enough to move the aspen leaves in a steady hiss. They stopped on the edge of a clearing in front of the house where once a lawn had been. Two magpies rose chattering from the side of the house and disappeared through the trees.

"Wildlife," said M. Chartier.

It was not a particularly large house, but a barn at the side and various outbuildings gave it a rambling effect. It looked in pretty good shape except where the ivy had dislodged some of the roof tiles on the barn.

Chartier had taken a bunch of steel keys from his pocket and as they crossed a concrete ditch he said, enigmatically, "The Germans."

But Sargesson hadn't heard him. He was already lost in calculations about the property. He was startled suddenly to hear his name called in the silence of the forenoon. When he looked up, Chartier had the door open and was waiting for him on the glassed-in porch.

From there double doors opened into a hall. Motes of dust moved endlessly in the beam from the fanlight, but otherwise Sargesson's first impression was that the place was unexpectedly clean and tidy. There was a stone staircase, a painted bamboo hatstand, and a chromium droplight with a beaded macramé shade. Although it must have been furnished after the war, it had the faint unreality of a theater set of the thirties.

The effect was enhanced when Chartier led him into a room on the right and opened the shutters noisily. There was more painted bamboo and an upright piano, which still had candle stumps in the sconces. Behind the doors was a hideous cocktail cabinet and radio-phonograph combined in yellow walnut veneer, and on top of it was a chromium salver with a cocktail shaker and a set of swizzle sticks in a tall drinking glass.

From alongside the French windows Chartier said, "It is just as she left it . . . about a year ago."

"The Marquise?"

"*Ah . . . non.* Not the Marquise." He didn't explain, just tilted his hand in the same ambiguous gesture. "A cousin . . . someone who came from Paris. *Très blasée.* They took some of the older furniture. A chest and some other things . . . antiques."

Sargesson moved back into the hall impatiently. On the telephone Chartier had told him there were cellars, and they were really the thing he was interested in. If they weren't okay, then it was a case of no deal. But when Chartier came out of the salon he went straight on up the stairs, and Sargesson had no choice but to follow. There were three bedrooms up there, a storage room, and an old-fashioned bathroom.

The main bedroom stank of old clothes and urine. Chartier put a handkerchief briefly to his nose while he opened the windows and shutters. "Of course this is just as it was left, you must understand. At the end I believe she was very old . . . without control. . . ."

There was gray hair and dandruff clogging the comb on the dresser and hooked to the bedpost was a short greasy crutch of pitch pine. Sargesson thought of her life there, of the pain and the misery and the humiliating incontinence, and unconsciously he compared it to the luxurious decline of Mrs. Wallace Grant in his own geriatric ward. On one of the windowsills where Chartier had opened shutters old geraniums had dried up in their pots as if all other life had departed with hers. He imagined the short, disgusted visit of the cousin from Paris, the car waiting in the drive . . .

As he went out into the corridor, Chartier banged the shutters closed and bolted them. From another window Sargesson saw the concrete ditch they'd crossed, which seemed to run along the eastern and southern boundaries, and now he noticed from his heightened vantage that there were two round disks of weathered concrete among the trees where they joined up.

"*Les Allemands.*" Chartier had come to his shoulder. And after a moment's reflection, he said, "It would be a splendid foundation for a summerhouse. . . ."

Weeks later, when Sargesson had been visiting the British Consulate, where they were giving a party for a brain surgeon from London, he had arrived early and spent half an hour in the Consulate library. A volume of the official history of the Strategic Air Offensive in World War II had been on one of the reading tables and he'd looked up Bellegarde in the index. The viaduct which had carried all the German traffic between France and the Italian front had been bombed on the fourteenth of September 1943 by a squadron of Lancasters from Spalding in Lincolnshire. A footnote to the raid said that the following day the German High Command had moved a flak regiment east from the naval base at Toulon to increase the defenses.

They stood at the foot of the cellar steps at last.

The air was musty and the reflection of M. Chartier's flashlight glared back at them from a pile of broken bottles. Workers from the Todt Organization, he explained, had carried out the fortifications. Ammunition had been stored there, and the gun crews had slept in the house.

"Enough storage space for a lifetime's wine," he added. His laughter clacked in the hollowness.

The beam moved on, lighting up graffiti which had been there since the war. But it was all on the same unvarying theme, penises like jumbo jets on takeoff with their scrotums unretracted and women's legs endlessly parted to reveal excrescences.

M. Chartier's tongue clicked.

"Can I have the light for a minute? I'd like to take a closer look."

Sargesson swept it over the ceiling, which was about eight feet high. The concrete still held the indentations of the staging planks. He moved down the short passage. There were two rooms off it, the doorways of which had dogleg walls to protect them from shock waves. He went into the first, and the flash wandered over a gray cell with more empty bottles in a corner.

Sargesson could hear M. Chartier breathing in the doorway behind him. He moved to the center and shook the droplight, releasing a shower of rust. He said, "All this will have to be rewired."

"Pardon?"

"I think I told you when I first called that stereo was something of a hobby of mine and I needed cellar space to make a good soundproof studio."

"Ah yes. The stereo."

Sargesson wandered back past the agent but didn't return the flash. He walked through a communicating door to the second room. There were broken pipes in the corner, the remains of some ventilating system, and more bottles. Sargesson was looking for a water pipe but there was none evident.

"And of course it would be an excellent place for the central heating boiler. . . ."

"Wouldn't that spoil the temperature of the wine?" Sargesson said, and imagined the little fat hand tilting this way and that in the darkness. As they moved back toward the steps, he felt as near exultation as it was possible for him to get. M. Chartier led the way out and they paused instinctively in the hallway with its hideous chrome droplight.

Sargesson said casually, "It's okay. I think I'll take it."

"And I think you are very sensible, Docteur. It is a type of property much in demand."

"What do we do now?"

"I will take from you the name of your *notaire,* you will sign a *soussigné,* an agreement with the person in Paris."

"How long before it's mine?"

"Two months perhaps."

"I'd like you to fix it as quickly as possible."

Looking beyond M. Chartier at the bamboo stand, he saw the reflection of his bleak face in the spotty mirror and turned away. To buy the house had been to turn a corner, and turning it he had come face-to-face with a stranger. He had seen, suddenly, the other man who was to live out whatever span of his life remained.

They went around the outside of the house before leaving. There was a small outbuilding on the western side where they hadn't walked before, and the striations of an old vegetable garden were still visible behind a screen of lilac and buddleia. A row of vines, untended for years, made a rambling hedge at the end farthest from the house.

M. Chartier's delicate town shoes kicked lightly at a long row of old chrysanthemum clumps. "For *le Jour des Morts,*" he said in a hushed respectful voice. "Flowers for the tomb." Even the dead were not beyond his reach and must contribute their mite to a successful deal. Sargesson would have free chrysanthemums for All Souls' Day.

He thought briefly of the little bed of marble chips that covered Marion in the cemetery at Caucade. He never took flowers. They were as ephemeral as her own short life had been. But someone else had put flowers there once. He had thought at the time it was Kemp or maybe one of her girl friends from school.

Walking back to the car M. Chartier continued to praise the thrift of French gardeners who grew flowers among the leeks and brussels sprouts, an economy for both the living and the dead. But Sargesson had stopped listening. The man who would have listened three months ago had died when Marion died.

Almost as if his thought had been audible, M. Chartier said, "The house is just for you, Docteur?"

"Yes," he said, and didn't know why he hesitated so long. "Just for me. My daughter died a while back."

By the time he got home the storm still hadn't broken.

Standing in the french window, Sargesson watched the ragged clouds charging eastward toward Monte Carlo and the Italian border. They were so wild and gaudy that he could almost feel the violence of their reflection on his skin. And to the west thunder and lightning circled the horizon like an artillery barrage. That was how it must have looked when the U.S. Seventh Army stormed ashore in 1944.

He had got back just in time.

To have been caught in the storm on the middle Corniche would have been the last straw in a day that had been pretty damn irritating. Sargesson's tall figure moved sticklike back down the room to the yellow walnut sideboard.

He made a drink, pouring jiggers of Cointreau and gin into the old-fashioned chromium shaker which had come with the house. He never used ice. Like a lot of medical men he had a few unscientific prejudices, one of which was that freezing drinks didn't do the alimentary canal any good at all.

He poured the cocktail into an ordinary café glass, dropped in a brown Greek olive, and left it to soak on the mantelpiece alongside the ormolu clock, which had also come with the house. Then he clicked on the stereo and turned over the half-dozen albums lying beside it before he picked up a selection of early Berlin played by the old Hamilton Boyd orchestra.

He left the room to the first notes of "Let Yourself Go."

In the hallway he stopped to tap the barometer that was hanging there, but it was right on the floor and didn't even flicker. He walked on in his jerky way with his wrists bent and his hands spread. (One of his friends at college, and it could only have been Tom Duffy, had said once that Sarge walked like a man who had just washed his hands and was looking for a towel.)

The cartons were on the kitchen table where he'd left them when he came in.

As he got a saw-bladed knife from the stove he couldn't remember which was which, only that they all had given him a really bad time ever since he'd picked them up in Nice during his lunch break. And cutting the string now had the same significance as cutting an umbilical cord after a difficult confinement. And, he thought dryly, it was certainly going to be some baby. . . .

The carton was custom-designed inside to hold trays of sliding plastic in a light frame. He untaped the first tray and as he slid it out a lot of frothy women's underwear was released. He picked a piece off the top at random and opened it out. It was a brassière, decorated with sequins and spangles, and the cups were open-tipped and as big and thrusting as pigs' snouts.

Sargesson's eyes widened. Then he said, "Jesus," in a deeply respectful voice.

He laid the bra aside and started to pick over the rest. There was a garter belt to match the bra and several pairs of black fishnet stockings, which like the bra were all monogrammed in *diamanté* with the letter *K*. He stuffed them back and cut the holding tape of the second tray, which was deeper than the others.

This one was full of footwear. There were shoes with platform soles and ankle straps, shoes with stiletto heels almost as sharp as needles, and two pairs of boots. One pair was jackboots and the other was more exotic, in shiny red plastic. The girl in the shop, he remembered now, had been wearing the red lacquered boots and practically nothing else.

The thought of the shop produced an immediate twitch of remembered fear and he turned abruptly and went down the hall for his drink.

The olive had done its work, leaving a small oil slick on the surface of it. He swallowed a mouthful, toasting himself in the ugly modern pier glass between the main windows. It had beveled edges and a really terrible zigzag design cut in one corner, but he had kept it, too, along with the chromium shaker and the rest of the junk.

The watchful eyes looking back at him were as bright

as the eyes of a marmoset, and with his deeply cleft cheeks and the soft lighting, he was looking more than ever like the sixteenth President. Marion had made the comparison after coming home from a history lesson, and even as he remembered it he turned away from the memory of her voice.

Thunder cracked across the sky, drowning out the light voice that was singing "The Piccolino," and a couple of seconds later thunder growled again. He turned off the music and freshened his drink from the shaker and took it back to the kitchen. In a recess on the mezzanine landing the telephone was tinkling, not the sustained rhythm of a call but the random ringing of a short circuit caused by the storm.

He cut the tape on the smaller of the two remaining drawers, which turned out to contain her jewelry.

It was laid out in compartments lined with black velvet, and the sudden vitreous glitter as he eased out the tray made him blink. There were bracelets and necklaces and a whole fistful of baroque rings. Alone in one compartment was a thigh garter studded with brilliants and in the center a demi-parure flashed with green and white fire. It was pinned to a cushion. Again the design motif was the letter K and although the effect was striking he knew they were only paste imitations.

He pushed the drawer shut and slit the tape that was securing the last one.

Two gilt cases were set into the top of the drawer. When he opened them, one held toiletries and the other cosmetics, laid out in rows like missiles. He lifted out the boxes and found other things lying underneath. There was a smell of new leather. The smell came from a kind of whip with a golden handle and a long sinuous lash of braided black suede. He stared down at it for a moment before snaking it to and fro over the table. It cracked with a kind of wet sound that was like a spoken obscenity in the room.

Underneath it was an armband with a swastika emblem in bright scarlet, and below that yet again a black skullcap in some kind of stretch fabric. When he turned it over in his hands he saw it had eyepieces like an executioner's mask.

There were two bulky plastic envelopes left. The first was neatly packed with a schoolgirl's leotard and a blue and white striped college scarf. He folded them neatly back into the envelope before he opened the second one. Slippery black satin fell through his hands, and for a moment he didn't know what it was. Then he saw it was a nun's vestment, open down the front. He recognized the habit of the Ursuline nuns who taught at the convent school on the outskirts of the town. The satin was difficult to fold, and in the end he rolled it into a ball and put it back in the envelope.

He pushed back the tray and picked up his drink. He walked back into the living room before he tasted it. The clouds were lower and darker and still flying eastward.

"Jesus," he whispered again. "What a kit!"

He hadn't realized, there in the shop, the scope of the purchase. In his hurry and embarrassment to get the business over with he had just counted out hundred-franc notes from the stack he had withdrawn from the Chase Manhattan Bank around the corner in the rue Grimaldi. All he had wanted was out and he hadn't really listened to what the highly scented girl in the red lacquered boots had been telling him.

Just about every fetish and sexual fantasy was covered by the gear in the box and some day he'd have to ask Josh Weiss precisely what some of them were all about. Josh was the consultant psychiatrist down at the hospital and he had been a great help around the time Marion died. He'd have to ask Josh. Standing there by the window in the yellow storm light, he drained his glass.

THE SOUND OF THUNDER ROLLING OVER THE TOWN WAS like shunted freight cars crashing together.

The wind was tearing at the house and bending the dark trees almost horizontal. A plastic fertilizer bag from God knows where flapped suddenly against the window for a moment before a sudden gust lifted it up and sent it sailing away into the night. Sargesson fixed himself another drink and left it with the olive soaking. He went back to the kitchen again. It almost took an effort of will, but the cartons had to be unpacked tonight. He wished he'd never gotten into this whole sexual thing, but since he was into it it would have to be gone through with. He started to open another, smaller, carton, slitting the tape carefully with the saw-bladed knife. Under the loose packing he could see an electrical appliance with a great coil of wiring wrapped around it. At first he thought it was some kind of an erotic instrument, some weird supplement to the gear in the first carton. But when he unwrapped the wire he found something like a portable hair drier.

He held it by the pistol grip, turning it over slowly. There was a heating element visible through a safety grill, controlled by a thermostatic switch. The switch meter rose from 35° to 45°centigrade, and there was a special red marker line at 37°, which was blood heat. There was also a clip-on barrel in the carton which fitted just where a pistol barrel would have been. The wire was three-way and taped at the end, and after he'd examined it he went to get his tool kit, which he kept in a corner of the cloakroom by the front door.

He came back and opened it up on the table and started taking a plug to pieces. He stripped the wire, threaded it into the terminals, and screwed it up again. Then he took the cord across to the percolator socket and plugged it in. Holding it by the pistol grip, he switched the motor on. There was only a faint whine from the fan and a stream of cool air. After a moment he turned the thermostat forward until it was set to full heat. He laid the thing down again, propping it against the side of the empty carton.

Then he stood there, feeling the air getting faintly warmer. He was holding his hands up loosely, palms toward his chest, as he sometimes held them in the surgery drier after scrubbing up before a minor operation.

He had forgotten all about his drink.

ON THE DAY AFTER MARION DIED HE HAD SURPRISED THEM
all by arriving at the hospital in the afternoon.

It was a Friday when he had no specific duties in the
morning, and he spent it, as he usually did such days,
slipping out early for the *Tribune* and then reading it
over coffee on the balcony outside the kitchen. After
that he called the staff nurse on Geriatrics to check on
one of his elderly patients, using the phone in his study,
which was farthest from Marion's bedroom.

Fran Olsen had sounded flustered when she heard
his voice and had told him not to worry.

"I'm not worried," he snapped. "I'd just like to know
how she is."

When he'd hung up, he continued to move quietly
around the apartment as he always did, waiting for her
to wake. Only then did he realize that the way he was
behaving was an involuntary denial of the facts, something which was part of the symptomatology of grief.
He went right on down the passage and opened the

door of her room. For a moment the familiar disarray, the half-made bed and the scattered clothes, revived his disbelief. But only for a moment. He closed his eyes painfully, still standing there near the doorway. After nearly half a minute he opened and closed his eyes again, but still no tears had come.

He went on standing there for a long time, opening and closing his eyes, like a man retching on an empty stomach.

When he got to the hospital he parked the Peugeot in the staff bay back of the dispensary and followed the path of golden gravel around to the front entrance. As the electronic door slid open and he went through, he was aware of a *frisson*, a moment's utter stillness, as the doorman and the girl at Reception stared at him. He stopped after a couple of paces to look back at the doorman and said, "I'm in attendance, Victor."

"Okay, Docteur. Okay."

Victor slid across the mahogany shutter that revealed his name in gold letters.

He walked on, entering the elevator on the heels of a young couple. "Second floor," he said when they looked at him. After they had thumbed buttons, they stood rigidly in a corner, immunized by their private anxiety.

He walked through to his office more slowly than usual, one half-spread hand carrying the key case. While he was unlocking his door, Ralph Bassadone came out of his own doorway farther up the hall.

Ralph called, "Sarge . . . ?" and added something he didn't hear.

He waved vaguely back and stepped into his room.

Standing against the door, he knew that either Victor or one of the girls on Reception had called up Ralph. He waited a quarter-minute but Ralph never came and he moved away, mechanically going through his usual routine. Jacket off, hand wash, a new starched white jacket from its wrapper. For a moment the air was sharp with a smell of chlorine. Then he stuffed his favorite old stethoscope into his pocket and, picking up the case notes file, he went out.

He went back downstairs and around to the Geriatric ward. Although his post was that of Senior Physician, the Geriatric ward was his special interest. Crossing the main vestibule again, he saw Robert Deschamps, the radiologist from Nice, but turned his head away quickly. He went past Reception and into the diary room. It had been his own innovation, when he was first appointed, that the front office keep an updated diary. Throughout the day it lay in the hatchway between the office and the diary room and was required reading by medical staff before going on duty.

It was important in a hospital of mixed nationalities, which was administered by a system of crazy committees, and where most of the doctors were courtesy staff, that everyone know what was going on.

As he reversed the book now, the girl who was drinking coffee in Reception gave him a petrified smile. He closed the hatch while he skimmed down the entries. Don Wilson, who was Chief Surgeon, had asked for a P.M. on Miss Street, a chest patient who had been with them about a month. Lieutenant Briscoe of the U.S.A.F., admitted after a car smash the previous day, was going out to Stuttgart base on an ambulance plane at eight o'clock that night. An anesthetist who had taken over from Jean Lacoste a week ago was staying on call for another week. Doctor Kemp and Doctor Bassadone were sharing the duty of Doctor Sargesson.

Sargesson drew a pen from his pocket and, glancing at his watch, wrote: 15.15 hours. Doctor Sargesson resumed his duties. He opened the hatchway again and put the book back.

He walked through to the Geriatric ward.

Standing at the door of the recreation room looking in, he was conscious of the delayed reaction while a couple of patients stared at him. Then one of them, a retired Englishman, said fruitily, "Good afternoon to you, Doctor."

He waved briefly before turning right and going into the office dispensary. Fran Olsen was making up some kind of chart. She said quietly, "Hello, Sarge."

"Hi, Fran." He closed the door precisely behind him.

"They said you were off duty."

"I put myself on again."

She had been on the staff almost as long as he had. Although most of the nurses were British, Fran had trained at the hospital of the University of Pennsylvania, where long ago he had done a stint as a resident. Touching the filing cabinet behind her, she said dryly, "There's a slug in the usual place."

He shook his head, and was relieved that this was as near to sympathy as she would get. He sat down.

He was still watching her and she smiled back. The smile deepened the diamond pattern of wrinkles around her eyes. She said, "Pete Kemp's been around; everybody's happy. So there's no sweat."

"Fine." He laced his hands behind his head, and they sat on in a silence that was relaxed. Somewhere in a distant room two girls were laughing, and nearby a phone buzzed twice and was silent.

Years ago he had been turned on by Fran, but it hadn't been a success for either of them. It was after one of the foreign consulate parties in Nice, of which there was an endless succession, and he'd dropped Fran off on his way home. Against all the rules he had gone up for a nightcap. He still didn't know exactly how they came to fall into bed, only that it hadn't worked out.

They had lain there for a drunken half-hour, failing to couple, before Fran had said in a voice that was as dry as her loins, "Sarge, let's not spoil a beautiful friendship."

After that they had dressed and gone out onto the terrace with a bottle of vodka and sat there through the long mild morning getting wiped out. The result of it all was that they had some kind of special relationship. He watched her restless hand turning a ball-point pen to and fro.

She said sadly, "Marion was here the day before yesterday . . . sitting right there where you are now."

He stood up and moved to the window. Below, the young couple who had shared the elevator with him were just coming out of the building opposite where the Prenatal Clinic was.

He said, "What did she want?" and was surprised at his own calmness.

"Oh, she often came by for some girl talk. She's had no one else much since her Mom left."

Sargesson noticed Kemp's old Bentley on the tarmac between the two buildings. It was parked at an angle, taking up enough room for about three ordinary cars.

He said, "Do you want to tell me what it was she talked about?"

"I don't think so . . . not if she didn't tell you herself." The phone buzzed and Fran dropped the ballpoint to pick it up. "Yes," she said, "he's here."

He took it from her. The receptionist said, "Mr. Barrymore to see you, sir."

"Who is it? Who is he? Has he a letter?"

There was a pause before she said, "It's personal, sir."

"Okay, take him up to my room. I'll be there pretty soon." He stood up and moved away over to the window. Again, his hands hung out as usual. He said, "Never, never change, Fran."

"Okay. I'll try and keep that breathless charm." It was the sort of conversation they often made, echoing old lyrics.

Then he said abruptly, "I'll be back around six," and went out.

Barrymore, when he saw him, was already a familiar figure, one of those people who were always smiling their way around the wards. He was gray at the temples and moved slowly, like a simpleton. He said now, as Sargesson stood just inside the doorway, "I think we met once before, Doctor Sargesson. My name is Barrymore but I'm not a member of that famous theatrical family. As a matter of fact, I'm a minister at St. Mary's Episcopalian Church in Villefranche. We share it with the Anglicans. I . . . I . . . I often think of the hospital here as part of my parish."

His black suit was shiny where his joints touched it and he had slight conjunctivitis. Sargesson went to his desk without speaking. After sitting down, he made a gesture for Barrymore to do the same.

"Well, now," Barrymore said, "it's about Marion." He put his fingertips together.

Sargesson turned his head away slightly and stared at a statistics chart on the wall beyond. He said, "Has someone asked you to come and see me . . . ?"

"Oh, no, sir."

Sargesson was silent, waiting. He watched Barrymore put his fingertips together again, as if it was necessary for him to complete some sort of circuit before he could speak.

"She told me, you see, that she wanted to be buried within the church."

"She told you *that*? Marion? When did she tell you that?"

"Well, if you want to know, Doctor, she had been to some of our little get-togethers at St. Mary's. Just lately, that is."

Sargesson was silent again, thinking over the last few months and everything she'd been doing. She hadn't told him about the church, maybe because they had never been churchgoing folk.

Barrymore went on speaking with a hesitation in his voice that was habitual, the result of continual extemporization. "She started to come and see us, oh . . . about a couple of months back. We had several uh . . . little talks."

"What about?"

Barrymore hesitated. "She was . . . she was in need of advice . . . of help, maybe from some extra dimension. . . ."

Sargesson said, in a voice that was harsh and disbelieving, "She didn't come to me."

He had said it too quickly, and the silence that followed seemed to spread slowly between them like a bloodstain growing on gauze.

In the end he had had to agree to a funeral at Caucade.

He didn't want to arrive early and have to speak to people in the hushed, furtive way they sometimes used at funerals, so he sat in his parked car half a mile from the entrance until he felt the service was about to begin. The day was unusually gray and misty and there was a cool moist wind as he walked up the path of white gravel to the small baroque chapel. As he drew closer he could hear the muffled singing.

> "Hear the voice forever calling,
> Who can know the joy in store!
> Take this loved one to Thy bosom,
> Comfort her forevermore."

One light tenor voice, that of Barrymore, he supposed, soared above the rest. He walked carefully through the doorway into the dimness and realized he was late after all. As the verses continued the bearers were leaving the altar, wheeling the pale coffin on a bier like some kind of dumbwaiter. He stepped into the last pew and stood with his head bowed, unwilling to meet their eyes as they went by him out into the grave-yard. When the last shuffling steps of the mourners had gone he turned and followed. Walking behind the small scattered group he saw several of the off-duty staff of the hospital were there. Fran Olsen was with Ralph Bassadone, and walking just behind the priest he saw Kemp following the limping figure of Josh Weiss.

Kemp turned once and looked back but without see-ing him. Sargesson saw he was wearing an old dark suit and a black tie. Even at a funeral Kemp managed to look *outré* and un-American, like some character out of Proust.

The short, untidy cortège turned left between a line of newer headstones and passed two French children arranging flowers on a grave. Beyond them, in the shel-ter of a blackthorn hedge, their mother was unpacking wine and food onto a red-checkered cloth. She seemed at home sitting there, as if the meal had become a common ritual. From ahead of him, Barrymore's voice floated back in snatches.

"Man that is born of woman hath but a short time to live, and is full of misery . . . and is cut down, like a flower; he fleeth as it were a shadow, and never con-tinueth in one stay."

Up ahead he could see the bier halted by an open graveside and the mourners gathering around it. The pale clouds were as close as a tent awning overhead and a sudden drift of wind scattered the blackthorn blossoms as it scattered Barrymore's words.

"In the midst of life we are in death; of whom may we seek for succor but of thee, O Lord, who for our sins are justly displeased?

"Yet, O Lord God most holy, O Lord most mighty, O holy and most merciful Saviour . . ."

With a slight shock Sargesson realized that the people ahead had left a clear path for him up to the grave. The bearers had taken tasseled ropes from beneath the trolley and were passing them under the coffin and lifting it away. Beyond the grave Barrymore stood alone, his surplice billowing in the wind and his small red-rimmed eyes staring back at Sargesson. His voice grew louder and more imperative.

". . . But spare us, Lord most Holy, O God most mighty, O holy and merciful Saviour, thou most worthy Judge eternal, suffer us not, at our last hour, for any pains of death, to fall from thee."

Several heads turned toward him, and for the first time he was conscious of the row of girls with eyes downcast above their college scarves. There was a boy among them with a pale, pointed face, and Sargesson realized all at once that they were from her class at school. While he still stood there hesitating, Barrymore's voice died away and more heads were turned toward him.

The bearers had lowered the coffin and withdrawn the ropes. Barrymore had advanced to the head of the grave; the clouds seemed closer and more suffocating. Then Kemp stepped up from the group ahead and bent to scoop up a handful of loose earth. As he let it fall on the casket Barrymore began to recite more rapidly than ever.

"For as much as it hath pleased Almighty God in His great mercy to take unto Himself our dear sister here departed, we therefore commit her body to the ground; earth to earth, ashes to ashes, dust to dust . . ."

Others followed Kemp, scattering earth and moving away. He was aware of a schoolgirl passing him, her face a rictus of grief, and Barrymore's voice hurrying on through the Collect.

Suddenly it seemed to be all over. Barrymore was walking through the headstones and one of the bearers had lit a yellow cigarette. Sargesson turned and found Josh Weiss waiting a few yards away from him. The others were already filtering off in different directions. He walked back down the center path and Josh limped along beside him without speaking. Josh was carrying a stiff foolscap envelope. The French family was repacking the basket, folding the cloth. There was a flower chain looped around the gravestone beside them, which he supposed the girl had made. They passed the chapel and continued down the main driveway, which was lined with cypresses, the tops already lost in the opacity of the silent mist.

As they went through the iron gates Josh said, "They say you're back at the hospital."

"Well, Josh . . . I thought it would be okay. Keep my mind off things. You know . . ."

"I don't want to sound smart, Sarge, but I don't think it's okay at all."

They followed the pavement around the crescent back toward where the cars were. Because of Josh's limp, their heels rang oddly on the quarter stones. Josh said dryly, "Not really the time to talk about it, I guess. But I dug up some papers for you to look at. Maybe you've seen some of them in the *J.A.M.A.* already." He pushed the envelope under Sargesson's arm. "I'd take the week off, Sarge. I really would."

He started to cross the road, skipping about to avoid the traffic. Sargesson went on until he came to his Peugeot and unlocked the driver's and passenger's doors automatically as if Marion were still with him. Sitting inside, he opened the envelope on his lap. There were Xeroxed copies of articles from the *Journal of the American Psychoanalytical Association,* as well as the *J.A.M.A.* He let the pages fall. Bloody Streeter he knew, and Max Klein and their theories. He regarded himself as already being well informed about the desirability of fully sublimated grief. He pushed the papers across to the passenger seat and started the car.

Suddenly he hated Josh and the whole fucking outfit. And with a rush he blamed Marion. Because she had taken the place of wife and daughter, she had now robbed him of both. He reversed violently out of the parking lot, the brakes shuddering as he stopped. The paper flew forward to the floor, fluttering around the gearshift. If he'd taken the time to read them he would have known, as Josh Weiss knew, that he was display-ing the classic manic defense that since the time of Darwin had been categorized as frantic grief. But Josh Weiss would never have guessed at the hate that stayed with him even while grief took its prognosticated course.

And grief, which should have become a cushion, became a goad, driving him farther into the shadows of a new and terrible life.

That night he had a nosebleed, but only a slight one, and pinching it in a cold compress checked it almost immediately.

It had happened regularly all through his adult life and was no more than an inconvenience which he'd learned to handle. The first one had been the worst and it had happened, oddly enough, on his honeymoon in Germany. The damn thing wouldn't stop, and in the end he'd gone to the hospital in Baden-Baden, where they'd cauterized the rupture.

The duty surgeon had been a red mountain of a man smelling of liquor and interested in the pathology of nosebleeds. "If no one hit you," he said, "what thing has been unusual?"

"Nothing unusual at all," Sargesson said. And, as a sort of wry joke, he added, "Except that I'm on my honeymoon."

"Ach so. . . . Then tell me, Doktor, are you a virgin?"

"Oh, for Christ's sake . . ." Sargesson laughed without humor.

The red face came suddenly closer to his. "But I was not joking, Doktor. . . . I was very serious."

IT MUST HAVE BEEN AROUND AUGUST, WHEN HE HAD BEEN in the new house only a couple of weeks, that he saw a stranger in the garden.

He'd just got back in the early evening and put the car away in the stable, and was walking back toward the house when he noticed a man crouched in the long grass against the wall by the kitchen garden. He felt an instant of panic, and as he drew nearer, irritation. The man was squatting beside a clump of young nettles carefully examining something. Although he had obviously heard the car arrive he still hadn't looked around.

Sargesson said sharply, "Have you lost something?"

"*Non, pardon . . .*"

The man twisted slightly, still sitting on his heels, and tugged a billfold from a pocket in his jacket. He had a creased face with a wide mouth and a broken nose and mild brown eyes, but the general effect was of a small boy. A tough small boy. Sargesson took the billfold calmly and, opening it, saw the *tricolore* and the battered face fixated in an I.D. photograph. The man's name was Auguste Peyrouse and he was an inspector from the Gendarmerie in Nice. As Sargesson passed the billfold back, he straightened up and took it.

"I should explain," he said. "I was looking for pupae ... they lay their eggs, butterflies, near a food source like nettles. I thought ..." He had a hobby to go with his small boy's face.

"What are you doing here, anyway?"

"I replaced Inspector Bouchet in the affair of the death of Elizabeth Marion Sargesson." He walked about youthfully as he spoke, his hands reversed on his hips. "The reason for my visit is really one of courtesy, Doctor ... to introduce myself and to assure you that the investigation concerning your daughter will continue. These things are a disgrace to France. Inspector Bouchet has taken statements from nine people, but the affair of your daughter seems to have been very discreet. There has been no firm evidence so far."

They had been walking back to the front of the house and now Sargesson said, "Where's your car?"

"I left it at the Gendarmerie in Bellegarde. I walked up from there. They told me which way to come to reach your house."

Sargesson had hoped Peyrouse would leave, but he stayed on, looking up at the front of the house. In the end Sargesson was compelled to say, "Can I offer you an apéritif?" He took out his key case.

"Oh no . . . thank you very much." Peyrouse hesitated. "If it is possible . . . I should like to wash my hands." He took them from his hips and held them out.

"You're welcome." Sargesson opened the door and walked into the hallway, which was still warm from the afternoon sun. He put down his medical case, and suddenly he saw the hall through Peyrouse's eyes, in all its faded period glory. He half-opened the door of the small cloakroom before he remembered that it was still stacked with books which the movers had left there. Peyrouse watched him, his battered face polite.

"There's a bathroom at the top of the stairs . . . first door on the right."

As Peyrouse ran lightly up, Sargesson went into the living room. Walking about uncertainly, he heard the water clanking in the pipes as Peyrouse turned on the taps. The room smelled stale, so he opened the french windows onto the garden, and then came back to the piano. He stood there with his eyes cast upward, waiting. Then, as if conscious of his nervousness, he moved over to the sideboard and opened one of the cupboards in it. He lifted up bottles of gin and whiskey and *pastis.* Then he took two glasses from the cupboard on the other side. He knew that Peyrouse would accept a drink at the second invitation, which was the French convention.

As he came back from getting ice from the kitchen he heard the lavatory flush. He walked back to the open window. It seemed to him that Peyrouse had had time enough to take a shower bath.

And then suddenly behind him the Inspector said, "Thank you, Doctor."

Sargesson turned around. He said, "Sure you won't join me?"

"Well, perhaps . . . a little Pernod . . ."

Sargesson poured a drink and added ice water. He said, "Why did you come here?"

"Pardon?"

Sargesson said, less sharply, "There was no need to come all the way out here. I'm at the hospital most days."

Peyrouse's shoulders lifted in a hopeless way. "I know . . . but you see most people do not like to have a policeman calling at the place where they work, and so I telephoned the hospital and asked where your new house was." He opened his newly washed hands in a gesture.

Sargesson poured himself a *pastis* but mixed it with water from the carafe. As he lifted his glass, Peyrouse did the same. Afterward there was silence for quite a time and the murmur of the aspens was audible through the open french window like distant breathing. Later he came to learn that Peyrouse's silences were a habit.

"Isn't it rather a long way to come to introduce yourself?"

"Perhaps," Peyrouse said, "but it is the usual thing. And I must confess something else."

"What's that?"

"I came also because I like an afternoon in the country. It is very restful after Nice." He cleared his throat. "And I have always liked Bellegarde very much. . . . It is a pity I may not have the opportunity to see it many times again."

"Why is that?"

"Shortly I, too, like Inspector Bouchet, may be reassigned. I am to go to a course of instruction at Grenoble."

The pipes shuddered noisily again somewhere in the house beyond, as the cistern finished filling. Sargesson emptied his glass and again Peyrouse followed him and finished his own.

Sargesson said, "We can use this door," and led the way out by the french windows.

As they reached the driveway, Peyrouse said, "Tell me one thing, Doctor . . ."

"What's that?"

"Do you have any dead bodies in your house?"

Sargesson froze. He was motionless for a moment before he turned toward his visitor. "What do you mean?"

Peyrouse wasn't smiling. But all the same, he said, "It was a joke, Doctor. When I washed my hands I saw the . . . the container of formaldehyde in your bathroom. Don't they use it to preserve bodies?"

Sargesson said, "Oh, sure. It's . . . what embalmers use. But in a weak aqueous solution it's also a great disinfectant. I can tell you, Inspector," he added lightly, "it's great for cleaning up old houses."

"Oh, I'm sure of that, Doctor." Peyrouse put out his hand. "Do not come farther. I can find my way."

Sargesson waiting saw him walk off down the drive taking long strides. He couldn't hear Peyrouse's footsteps. He must have had soft soles on his shoes.

He entered the house through the french windows

again and closed them behind him. He picked up his glass and mixed a fresh drink, and after he'd tasted it he left it on the piano while he crossed the hall and went upstairs.

In the bathroom, the hand towel was wrinkled where Peyrouse had dried his hands and hung it back on the rail. Sargesson looked around the room carefully before he opened the cupboard where the linen was stored, and then the mirror cabinet where his brushes and razor were kept. Then he bent to examine the small plastic drum of formaldehyde. There was a stick-on label across it. It said, "DROGUERIE CENTRALE," and below someone had written with a red ball-point, "Five litres, HCHO 40%."

Neither formalin nor formaldehyde was mentioned by name, so Peyrouse must have known the chemical symbol for them, or else he had unscrewed the cap and recognized the smell. If Peyrouse wanted to locate the Droguerie Centrale in Villefranche he wouldn't have much difficulty. Going back down the gloomy staircase, Sargesson decided that he wouldn't visit there again. He'd go somewhere else for the next lot. That is, if things worked out the way he planned.

Picking up his drink again, he remembered that it was Thursday and that he had only half an hour before it was time to change for his visit to the Coq Bleu.

He drove on the middle Corniche, where the traffic was thinner at night.

It was a month back, before he moved, in fact, when he first started visiting the Coq Bleu, which was between the Château and the Place Masséna in one of the little streets running out of the Promenade. Tourists used it mostly and visiting executives with sharklike faces and no manners.

Fountains played among potted palm trees in the foyer and a faint oversweet smell like attar of roses permeated every corner of the place. In the main salon a pianist and his small group wore long-plumed head-dresses which nodded to the beat of the music. The girls were topless with see-through harem trousers. They were as sleek and spangled as well-drilled circus ponies. He had met most of them over the first couple of weeks as they rotated dutifully among the tables. They were all polite and, sitting in the dimness, almost indistinguishable, just an impression of petrified hair and big breasts with nipples like bruises. And they had all adopted the names of movie stars like Marlene, Judy, and Marilyn.

Except for Momma Fritz. "Because I come from Hamburg . . . someone called me that," she said in her deep voice.

Unlike the others', her blonde hair was lank and circled her face like giant fangs. "It was on the first day . . . no, the second. And I've been Momma Fritz ever since. I don't care, actually."

"I don't care, actually" was one of her catch phrases, picked up from an early English lover. It was her inevitable reply to a hundred different questions. She had small gray eyes and a mouth as hard and bright as the lips of a conch shell.

"Why did you leave Hamburg?"

She shrugged. "I left."

On the first night he had drunk *pastis.* The turbaned waiter had said it was impossible, and some kind of headwaiter had to be consulted.

"They want you to drink the champagne," Momma Fritz said.

"Would you like that?" he asked.

"I will have *pastis* too. Fuck them." It was another expression learned from her English lover.

After that the *pastis* was allowed, but only as a special concession, the headwaiter had impressed on him. At four dollars a shot it was some concession, he thought.

On the next night Momma Fritz had come to his table again, putting down, in a proprietorial way, the small sequined clutch bag which held her cigarette case and lighter. After that it became a routine. He always arrived early, soon after eleven, and left around one or two, when the tables were starting to fill with tourists from the big hotels along the Promenade. After he'd been there three or four times, another night when she'd been more alive than usual, teasing him about a new tie he had bought ("It's quite unnoticeable . . . it is very British. I don't care for it actually") she suddenly knocked her lighter from the table. Before he could pick it up for her she had slipped from her chair to search for it. The instant she was under the table he felt her hand lightly brush his genitals. It was a feather touch, like the hand of a blind man. Then she was back in her chair again.

Before she spoke she carefully fitted a cigarette between her gastropoid lips and lit it. Then she said, "What do you want, my Sarge . . . what thing? Why do you come here? You don't want me, that's for sure."

"I don't know," he said.

"Why do you come here?"

"For your company, I guess. I don't know. . . ."

"I don't know what I want either. . . . I don't care, actually." She stretched then, showing her unshaven armpits, the blonde hair dark with sweat.

Later, when they had drunk a little more, she talked about a day, a memorable day, when a friend had flown her to Casablanca for lunch. She had told him about it before and she, too, must have remembered then, because suddenly they were both bored. Then Momma Fritz said, "It isn't true that I don't know what I want. I do know what I want, actually."

He didn't say anything, and she looked away around the room. "I want peace."

She said it without sentimentality. "Peace . . . that is all."

"I want peace, too," Sargesson said and knew that he was a little drunk. For a moment he had sounded like a goddam evangelist.

"I mean," said Momma Fritz in a businesslike voice, "I mean I want a properly negotiated peace . . . with God and with my family. But I am now in a very weak position to negotiate."

He never knew what impulse made him reach into his pocket for the locket. "I want you to have this," he said and laid it in her upturned hand.

"Oh Sarge . . ."

"I really mean it," he said.

He saw the tears on her lashes and before she could say anything else he left.

Tonight he parked on the Promenade, where there was a lot of space as usual, and he stood for a while watching the moon path that ran across the Bay of Angels toward the lights of Antibes.

He was still on the early side so he walked around the long way past the Palais de Justice. The place was almost empty when he got there, and after he'd sat around for a while and she still hadn't come he signaled to one of the other girls. Her name was Jackie, he remembered, and she had been a friend of Momma Fritz's for some time.

"Where is she?" he asked. "Why isn't she here?"

"She go."

"Go? Go where?"

Jackie shrugged and beckoned a waiter for champagne. Sargesson waited irritably while the ice bucket was wheeled up to their table, the bottle was twirled and the cork popped and Jackie swallowed the obligatory mouthful.

"How long has she gone for? When is she coming back?"

"Not back here. She takes all her things." Jackie cupped a hand under one breast and smiled her vacant smile. He got up and left.

On the way out there was a man, some sort of manager, who always stood near the ticket booth. He had a pitted face and oiled hair and he wore evening dress.

Sargesson said quietly, "I'm looking for Momma Fritz."

"She gone." When he smiled he showed one dark gold tooth. "Plenty more," he said and made as if to lead Sargesson back.

"I'm just leaving," Sargesson said. "Do you happen to know where she's gone?"

"Maybe back to Naples."

"But she came from Hamburg."

The man shrugged and tilted his hand this way and that. There were tufts of black hair covering his knuckles. "Plenty more girls," he said again.

Sargesson went down the steps into the hot night where cabs were swarming. He walked through them back toward the Promenade. He was glad he had spoken to the man in the foyer, and Jackie. If something terrible had happened to her they would know it had nothing to do with him. The floor manager, or whatever he was, would remember that he had been surprised and concerned.

It was as if he were insuring himself in some way, as if it were some kind of rehearsal for future guilt.

7

SARGESSON HAD TURNED OFF THE AIR PUMP, PUT IT BACK IN the carton, and finished his drink.

The storm was right over the house now, the thunder and lightning, almost simultaneous, was deafening, and the first great drops of rain were like stones thrown at the window. He had begun to cut through the tapes of the last carton, which meant cutting around the whole package, almost. He'd realized at the time that the bitch in the shop had been deliberately slow in wrapping it up, as she'd been slow about everything else.

Looking back on it now, he realized that the discomfort of her customers was probably what gave her kicks. The interview room was one of several off an antechamber which in turn was off a shop where the Niçoise bourgeoisie went constantly in and out, buying contraceptives and other sexual necessities. The whole place had been pretty hammy, and the girl hadn't sat behind her desk but on it, swinging one of her red

lacquered boots. She was also wearing dark glasses, as
he was, and as did pretty well most of the people who
went there, he guessed. It was so quiet in the room that
he could hear his own breathing.

"*Pas de négresses grandes,*" she had said. "We have
no big black girls remaining . . . only the small sizes."
She was apologetic, like a waitress explaining that the
filet steak was out.

Then she had thumbed a button on her desk panel,
illuminating a showcase that ran the length of the wall.
The negress, who had a fine brown body, was between
an oriental and a Swedish-looking blonde. They were
all narrow-waisted, with big hips and big breasts. The
blonde girl had high cheekbones and concave cheeks
and lips like squashed raspberries.

To the right of the group was the figure of a boy. He
had rosy lips, too, pouted rosy lips and silken lashes,
the caricature of a catamite.

The girl must have seen him looking at the boy, as
she said, "You would prefer a boy? He is . . . he is quite
complete. . . ." She hesitated again, trying to remember
the English idiom she had been taught. "Anatomically
correct?" she said at last, but still with uncertainty in
her voice.

"No, thank you. I don't want a boy."

"You are not a priest?"

"No," he said loudly, although he was quite aware
that his ascetic face with its clawed cheeks gave him
the faint look of a hell-fire preacher.

"The boy is very popular with the priests," the girl
said seriously.

"I'll just take the blonde model," he said. And he added, "As a matter of fact it's for a friend . . . a kind of joke, I guess. . . ."

She didn't turn off the showcase lighting and she didn't move. She just sat there with her boot swinging, a pendulum that ticked off the seconds of his embarrassment. "The correct size is very important. How tall are . . . is your friend?"

"Around one meter eighty, eighty-five maybe . . ."

"Then the correct size would be the one meter seventy-five size," she said pedantically.

Again there was silence and the swinging boot glinted in the muted light.

Behind him someone had entered the outer showroom. Whoever it was had shoes that creaked slightly as he moved around on the soft carpet examining the massage vibrators, the rubber clothes, and all the other display material.

Then the girl said, "There are certain accessories which it is important to buy, as they are purpose made by the manufacturer. They are . . ."

"I'll take the accessories," he said abruptly.

She picked up the telephone at last and murmured rapidly in French to someone in the stockroom out the back somewhere. Then she went behind the desk and started to tick off the boxes on an order form. Sargesson was conscious of the man waiting in the room behind. Now he could hear the slight scraping as the pages of a catalogue were turned. He hoped that the girl wasn't going to go all through it again.

She looked up and smiled at him. "Would you like a

cigarette?" A small panel opened automatically in the desk in front of him. It was filled with gold-tipped cigarettes. As he shook his head, the lid slid noiselessly back.

The girl said, "It will not be a very long time. Cash, credit card, or check?"

"Cash."

She finished writing out the order form, tore off two carbon copies, dropped one down a chute in the desk and passed the other over to him. He got out the wad of hundred-franc notes which he'd just taken out of the bank. Counting them, he realized that it came to almost a thousand dollars. Before he finished, a man in a warehouse coat came through with the three cartons and the girl began to tape up the seams.

"You are on holiday?"

"Well, kind of . . ."

"The Côte d'Azur is very beautiful at this time of year."

"It surely is."

As the small talk went on, he laid the notes in front of her, hoping that this might speed things up, but she merely picked them up and put them aside. The man in the anteroom cleared his throat and afterward started up a tuneless whistle between his teeth.

Sargesson said, "I'm sure they'll be okay. I don't have far to go."

"It's no trouble." Picking up the third carton, she said, "We have many American customers. You are from America?"

"That's right."

"My aunt is married to an American in Plainview. Do you know Plainview?"

"Well, I've heard of it but I've never been there. Look, that's fine, really . . . I don't have too much time. . . ."

She finished taping at last and began counting the money deftly. He had loaded the cartons up before she was through. The man in the anteroom was young and tall, wearing dark glasses as well. He didn't look away when Sargesson came out, but smiled easily, without embarrassment.

Sargesson followed the rue du Congrès and picked up a cab near the Promenade, giving the address of the hospital. When they arrived he directed the driver around to the parking lot at the back, and it was only when he got there that he found they hadn't brought his car back from the body shop. He paid off the driver and took the cartons up to his office, fending off the orderly who offered to take care of them for him.

For the rest of the afternoon he was troubled by the memory of the young man who had been waiting. It was the sort of shop that cops would keep an eye on. He was haunted by the young man's confident smile just as he was haunted by the smell of musk which still clung to his clothes beneath the hospital jacket.

Sipping a White Lady, he could smell it still as he stood watching the raindrops dancing a foot high off the windowsill. Swirling gusts of rain obscured the trees on the other side of the garden and the sound of it almost blocked out the rolling thunder. It had been raining only fifteen minutes, but already a sheet of water covered the driveway, which was just visible in the gloom of the storm.

It had taken him fifteen minutes to inflate the exotic figure now reclining on the chaise longue. The inlet valve had been set cleverly between two center toes and was so small that he would never have found it without the help of the diagram in the carton. He supposed that this was about as remote from an erogenous zone as you could get. He had set the dial at maximum temperature and as he triggered in the hot air the latex skin had slowly unwound from around the articulated joints and expanded to the same voluptuous proportions as the model in the shop. He moved away to draw the floor-length curtains before turning on the lights.

She could have been a patient lying there in the dimness of the chaise, one elegant hand with its carmine nails thrust upward toward her head, and as he went to sit alongside her he could have been back in his consulting rooms at the hospital. He took her arm to return it to her side and it moved easily, like the universal joint on a modern doll. Then he pinched her belly lightly, like a French housewife pinching a capon at a market. She was warm to the touch, though, and as firm as when he had first inflated her.

With the same detachment as he would have handled the limbs of a patient, he straightened and slightly parted her legs. He examined a foot first, pressing and bending it. The ankle joint was simple and allowed only backward and forward movement, but the texture of the calf was firm, almost as if there were tendons there. He twisted a knee gently and it had slight lateral movement as well, due to some kind of ball joint, he guessed. The upper leg, when he moved it, had the same kind of mobility. He pressed the thigh and felt faint corrugations under the skin like the striations of a muscle. It was not for the sake of reality, though, but a piece of functional design, he decided. Maximum friction would occur between the legs.

He flicked the pale pubic hair and his fingers probed the vagina and the anal passages briefly, and there was no doubt about it; the original molding had been made from a life model. The whole perineum was perfectly reproduced. There was white powder on his hand when he withdrew it from the crotch.

Looking up into the sulky, sexual face for a moment, he almost said, "Let me know if I'm hurting you."

Outside in the growing darkness the rain had begun to ease, and the sound of it was now light and only just audible. His hands moved upward, gently pressing her abdomen and her breasts. Again the skin seemed to be reinforced and the nipples had the integumental solidity of fingertips. He put a hand to the point of her jaw and moved her head slightly toward him. Through a curtain of lashes one turquoise eye seemed to look limpidly back at him. With its pupil and iris correctly set in depth, it was as accurate a reproduction as the pelvis had been. Holding the head, he moved it firmly on the spinal axis, first from side to side and then up and down. The blonde hair was as fine and soft as the flow of water across his hands. He lifted it away to look at her ear. Even the auditory channel was there, though it didn't go in very far.

He left her head tilted back, making shadows of the concave cheeks, and pressed gently on the scarlet mouth. As his fingers penetrated into the orifice behind, he felt the shape of jaws pressing on them. The teeth were soft and cartilaginous like the nipples, and the whole mouth right back to the fauces had a spongy, membranous quality.

He stood up abruptly and walked away with his hands hanging. Automatically he crossed the hall to the cloakroom and washed, as he always did following an examination. Standing before the mirror, he remembered the slight elasticity of the anal and oral sphincters and the exactness of the cavities behind, and it was obvious that just as the wardrobe had catered to a variety of sexual fantasies, so the body itself was capable of numerous perversions. He dried his hands with care.

Beyond in the night, the rain had stopped and the eaves were dripping. The thunder was distant, away to the east, somewhere in the Gulf of Genoa.

AFTER THE CONTRACT WAS COMPLETED AND THE NEW house was finally his, he had written to one of the smaller security companies with an office in Nice.

He had used embossed hospital writing paper and signed the letter in his capacity as Senior Physician. Later, on the phone, he explained to M. Vivier, one of the executives, the exact nature of what was required. So they had met late one afternoon at a café in Bellegarde. M. Vivier was middle-aged and laconic. He had a bleached, sandy look and a slight scoliotic twist to his neck, which gave him an attitude of permanent inquiry. They drank a *pastis* outside in the weak sunlight, while Sargesson explained further.

"The whole thing is very much in a minor key because we don't have the funding of big institutions, but in the remote event of hostilities on the European continent, we would just like to have our archives secured. We've located this place, which is halfway to what we need already. All we want really is the electrical and ventilation systems brought up to date and the proper doors installed."

"Ah, oui." M. Vivier appeared a little disappointed, possibly at the size of the contract. His attentive attitude relaxed slightly; his stoop became a little less pronounced.

"It's not far," Sargesson said, "just a kilometer up the road. And it's an old house which was a German garrison post during the war."

"Ah, oui."

They drove up there through the sun-flecked avenues, taking both cars after a mild altercation about who would ride with whom. There were still tall weeds in the forecourt and the house had a blank untidy look. When M. Vivier appeared from behind his car he was wearing a helmet and yellow boots and carrying a tool kit. They went inside and straight down to the cellars, M. Vivier tapping and examining the walls as he went. In the gloom at the bottom of the steps he produced a flashlight so powerful the reflection of it off the walls blinded them both for a moment. Then Vivier led the way briskly through the small complex, the beam of the flash roaming the walls and ceiling as they went.

It lingered once or twice on the graffiti and each time M. Vivier said dryly, *"Formidable."*

Back at the stairway again, he shone the beam between their feet while he talked. "I cannot commit myself, of course," he said, "until a complete examination has been made, but the existing structure seems to be a good basis. May I return here with my assistant during the week, after which visit I can submit a plan?"

"That's fine. Do you mind if we clear up a few points now?" Sargesson looked down at his own rather tired suede shoes confronted by the yellow boots gleaming with efficiency. "We do want some special arrangements that make for easy inspection and so on." In general he explained what was wanted. "I have a couple of drawings upstairs. You can take them with you."

"*Ah, bon.*" The yellow boots moved away and the flash went out. Sargesson followed him up the stairs.

A week later the estimates were in his hands, and they were about twice as much as he could afford. After combing through them, he cut out the drainage system, which accounted for nearly half of the fifteen thousand dollars. Levels were responsible for this item, wrote M. Vivier, and orthodox layouts were not possible. Therefore they were recommending an electrical pumping system with a kind of gravity ram as a backup.

Sargesson called him up then and there. "Something has to give," he said reluctantly. "So I guess we'll have to cancel the drainage item."

"You realize, Doctor, that your installation will not then qualify for the guarantee against flooding?"

"Okay. We'll have to risk that." There was silence for a minute. Sargesson imagined Vivier's slightly twisted head with the telephone tucked behind his clavicle. "I'd like you to get on with it as fast as you can."

"It will, of course, have the other guarantees against nuclear fallout, burglary, fire."

"That's great. Now if you will excuse me . . ."

After he'd hung up, he made a note in the desk diary to call up M. Vivier in a week's time and check on progress. When he flipped the pages back, he noticed it was Thursday and that Kemp was going to give him a lesson on the Bentley.

He started going out to Bellegarde on weekends.

There was a cement mixer standing in the forecourt, and the builder had stacked a lot of things in the barn. Vivier had told him that most of the equipment, things like the steel doors and the air conditioning unit, were coming out of stock and the contractor would be through within a month.

Two ventilator pipes had been raised unobtrusively to the eaves in a recessed corner of the west wall and one evening when he was there earlier than usual he met the foreman, a small morose man. He was seated at a scrubbed table in the kitchen filling in time sheets for the week. On the table, corked with a piece of cotton rag, there was a bottle of *rouge*, which he offered Sargesson.

Sargesson said, "Thanks," and the foreman took two glasses to the sink, rinsed them, and filled them. They toasted each other formally. The wine was soft and slightly bitter in the mouth, the sort of wine Sargesson was always being offered but never seemed able to buy himself.

The work was going well. "No problems," the foreman said sadly, almost as if it was a matter of regret. They would be finished with the cellars in a week and could then start on the rooms above. They had walked into the living room by now, and the foreman began to look less morose at the prospect of getting his hands on it.

"I'm not doing anything else," Sargesson told him, "just updating the plumbing and electricity. I'm keeping the place the way it is."

The foreman turned away, a hand scratching his head, maybe to hide his astonishment. Sargesson knew it was crazy and knew that his voice had sounded odd and strained. He thought he knew the reason, too, but it was so convoluted that he wasn't really sure. The foreman shrugged and moved back to the kitchen.

Following him, Sargesson said, "There is one thing. . . . I'd like you to leave me a bag of cement and fifty kilos of sand out in the barn."

"Certainly, M'sieu. Good night." The foreman gathered his papers and went out to the waiting pickup. He waved carelessly as he drove off.

Sargesson went down to the cellar, avoiding another bottle of *rouge*, which was standing on the stairs. He walked around, the loose sand grating under his feet. There were patches of wet cement where they had hung the runners for the steel doors and sunk mountings for the ventilator unit. It was all just the way he'd planned. It smelled pretty dank in there, and after a moment he went upstairs again.

That night he phoned the *Nice-Matin* and placed an advertisement offering his old apartment for sale. They promised it would appear the following Saturday.

He hadn't put a telephone number in the advertisement because he liked his line always to be open in case of some emergency call from the hospital.

The *Nice-Matin* was mailing the replies. He was faintly disappointed on the Monday that there was only one, but the reason was, he saw, that it had been sent to the newspaper on Saturday night by hand. It was from someone called Miles Meredith, saying he would like to view the place as soon as possible and giving a Cannes telephone number.

When he dialed it from the hospital and asked for Mr. Meredith, a crisp voice corrected him. "Major Meredith speaking." He had a British accent and he said, "We would like to view the apartment today . . . if we can."

"That's not possible. I shan't be home until seven."

In the end they agreed that Meredith would call around eight o'clock. Now, as he waited, Sargesson went from room to room, putting books back on shelves and generally getting the place into shape, the way it had always been when Marion was alive. Right on time the door knocker banged twice, and when he opened the door there were two men there.

The Major was tall, with darkish gray hair and a gray suit. He wore a regimental tie. He said, "I'm Meredith and this is Jeremy Stuart . . . a friend of mine. Kind of you to see us so quickly."

"That's okay, Major." He stood aside for them and said, "Go straight ahead. The living room is right at the end."

As Stuart went by him Sargesson saw that he was wearing a kind of short bolero shirt under his flared denim suit and that his midriff was quite bare. He was also pretty well armored with beaten silver ornaments. The Major went straight to the window, surveyed the soft rose-colored rooftops which sloped away to the sea just visible through the evening haze.

He turned around and said, "What do you want for it?"

"Well, I thought around three hundred thousand francs."

"How many bedrooms?"

"Four. But I have one as a kind of study."

"That sounds perfect. Perhaps we had better look at it first."

They trailed politely after him through room after room. At the doorway of Marion's room he felt some comment was necessary. "This was my daughter's room."

After a pause, the Major said, "Quite charming."

Jeremy Stuart went to the window and opened it. He said, "Is there a way up to the roof?"

"You can get up there from the next floor, but there's only room for a clothesline. We . . . I've never used it."

"Must have that," said Stuart, "for Morgan to pursue his *amours.*"

"What a hideous expression, Jemmy."

"Sorry."

"We are a *ménage à trois,* Doctor. We have a blue Persian."

Going back along the corridor Stuart said, "The warming cupboard . . ."

And Major Meredith echoed, "Oh, yes . . ."

Sargesson went back to open the walk-in closet beside

the bathroom. There was a hot-water tank there, with shelves for linen alongside. Stuart bent down to it. Looking up at Sargesson, he said seriously, "It's for drying my strawberry leaves."

"Jemmy makes metheglin . . . a sort of mead."

"The nectar of the gods!" Stuart said indignantly.

"Only rather decadent gods. . . ." The Major smiled at Sargesson. His gray eyes seemed to be constantly full of challenging humor. They moved back to the front room and the view of the rooftops. "I wonder if you'd mind, Doctor . . . before we haggle, can Jemmy and I look around together? It's a question of seeing whether Lares and Penates, those rather more domestic gods, can be fully accommodated."

"Go right ahead."

Sargesson waited by the window, hearing them moving from room to room and the quiet murmur of their voices. He heard the lavatory flush in the bathroom and a moment later the faucet running. As he moved idly back toward the door, he heard Stuart speaking. "Yuckey yuckey."

The Major replied, "Oh, it's not so bad . . . quite a nice bit of tat really." They came back at last and from the doorway the Major said, "I have to tell you that we like it very much. Don't we, Jem?"

"Yes. Super."

Sargesson said, "Fine." He moved around to the corner cupboard. "Can I fix you a drink? We may as well be comfortable. . . ."

"Have you sherry?"

Jeremy Stuart sat Pan-like on the floor with his back

against an occasional table. Meredith, sitting in a wing chair, said, "Do you mind a pipe?"

And when Sargesson said, "No, sir," he laid it on the table in front of him. From another pocket he took a pouch which bore the same regimental colors as his tie, and from another pocket a box of wax matches. He was like a man turning out his pockets for a customs inspector. Filling his pipe methodically, he said, "We'd like it but it really needs redecoration and a few other things doing to it. Would you accept two hundred and eighty?"

Sargesson hesitated. "Well, now . . . these are early days, Major."

The Major sipped his sherry, holding his pipe poised. The stem was gray around the mouthpiece with the baked alkali from his saliva. "I suppose that's true," he said and started to light it.

For the first time Sargesson noticed that Jeremy Stuart had some sort of jewel or sequin in his navel. As he twisted to put down his glass it flickered like a heliograph winking from some frontier post. Jeremy Stuart said, "Let's take it, ducks."

The Major looked across at Sargesson, his eyes filled with helpless amusement again. "It seems I have no choice. Shall we agree at that?"

"Okay with me," Sargesson said. He was relieved that it had all been so quick and easy. Maybe he should have asked more.

Jeremy Stuart emptied his glass, and as he stood, the heliograph flashed another signal from his tanned belly. He was making the decision to move as he had

made the decision to buy the apartment and as he had
seemed to make other decisions. Standing, the Major
wrote the name of Sargesson's lawyer in his notebook.
"We'll leave it all to the *notaires,* shall we? And ask
them to settle it as soon as possible."

"That's fine with me."

Then, at the door, just as they were leaving, Jeremy
Stuart said, "Why are you leaving, Doctor?"

Sargesson hesitated. "My daughter is no longer
here," he said. "It's bigger than I need."

After they'd gone he walked from room to room the
way they had done. It was then he decided that apart
from his books and records he would sell most of the
things. They belonged to the old life he was leaving
behind. And he would keep the new house pretty much
the way it was, even though it might be a bit eccentric.

He did not yet admit to himself that apart from the
cellars, which were essential to his new abode, the
decor of the place also had a special meaning for him.

THE DAY THAT MARION DIED WAS A THURSDAY AND A DAY
when he had normal duties.

She was finishing a hurried breakfast when he came
out of the bathroom and went to get coffee for himself.
Afterward he couldn't remember what her mood had
been, whether she had been happy or sad, or even what,
if anything, they'd talked about. He'd taken his coffee
into the bedroom to drink while he was dressing and he
hadn't seen her again. There had just been the usual
cry in the hall, " 'Bye, Pop," and the slam of the front
door.

The shock had come about four when he was in the
Therapy ward. First an emergency call for him on the
intercom, and then when he got to Reception, Ralph
Bassadone was waiting with concern in his eyes.

"It's Marion, Sarge. . . ."

"Marion?" For a moment he thought only of some
patient. "Marion?"

"She's been admitted to the casualty department at

Menton . . . the Bon Secours. Would you like someone from the pool to drive you . . . ?"

"But Marion's at college. There's some mistake . . ."

"I don't think so," Ralph said seriously. "I don't think there's any mistake."

"Marion?" he said again, trying to think what Ralph was telling him.

"Can I have your keys, Sarge? Gauron or one of the boys will get you over there much quicker than you can drive yourself."

"They're in my desk, I guess. I'll get them."

As he made for the stairs and went swiftly up, two or three at a time, he heard Ralph telephoning for a driver. There was someone waiting in his outer room, some woman he hadn't seen before, and he went straight through to his office, stripping off his hospital jacket as he moved. He put on the light mohair coat hanging behind the door, got his keys from the center drawer of his desk, and went out again. The woman, still sitting there with a tote bag at her feet, gave him a watchful smile. He went down to the hall, one half of his mind aware of the tension there, the other half trying to rationalize the situation. The odds were pretty much against its being Marion, but even if it was he had to remember that the Bon Secours was a good hospital and she'd be in very good hands.

Ralph joined him on the move and they went down the back corridor and out to the parking lot. Ralph held his arm. "Gauron says it'll be quicker in an ambulance because they'll give him priority."

"Is it the place above the bay? Tall and white?"

"That's right. We played tennis there last year. I don't know whether you . . ."

"No, I didn't go." Out in the cool spring air Sargesson saw Gauron waiting by a Citroën. The blue light was flicking.

Ralph said, "I'll come with you if you want. . . ."

"No need. I'm sure everything will be okay." He looked around vaguely, only half-aware of the oleanders and the cold brilliance of the afternoon. "Everything will be okay," he repeated.

He sat in the car and looked straight ahead. Gauron had gone around to the driver's seat and Ralph now held the door, hesitating. Eventually he closed it and stepped away.

Gauron drove swiftly and as they slid around the quay toward the middle Corniche, Sargesson took his notebook from his pocket and looked briefly at his appointments for the rest of the day and for two or three days following. There was nothing among them that couldn't be postponed or couldn't be handled by somebody else with a little switching around.

Not that the situation would arise. And again he muttered, "Everything's going to be okay." By an effort of will he kept the phrase echoing in his mind. It wasn't *his* Marion, of course. Later, when they were up on the Corniche, near Eze, he tried to figure out different answers to account for the mistake in identification. One, Marion had lent a school notebook to a friend, it had her name in it. . . .

At the end of the Corniche, as they swept along the palm-fringed beach road, Gauron lifted an arm to point ahead. The hospital was up there, glittering among the trees, and he could see the *tricolore* drooping at the masthead over the cupola of the main building. He was out of the car before Gauron had snapped on the handbrake and walking swiftly toward the entrance.

At the reception desk he waited impatiently for an elderly German who was asking about the price of something. When he could wait no longer he said, "I'm Doctor Sargesson from the American hospital in Villefranche."

"Ah, good afternoon, Docteur. . . ." The receptionist smiled. "Doctor Vallier's expecting you. You are to go to the operating room. I shall send for a guide. . . ."

"There's no need. I'll find it."

"Follow the corridor to the right. It is in the next block. . . ."

With a wave of his hand he was walking away before she'd finished. Going down the corridor he remembered her smile. Hope, one of the emotions he had long ago forbidden himself, returned regardless. The girl would not have smiled if it had been *too* serious. Marion was okay. Following the arrow, he went out through electronic doors and across a covered path toward the next building.

Inside the building he took the corridor which said "Medical Staff Only," and after passing a couple of lateral doors he came to a cut-off with warning lights. The orderly was reading a paper opened out across a gurney. He folded it as Sargesson approached.

"I'm looking for Doctor Vallier."

The porter pointed to the red panel. "He is still working."

Sargesson said anxiously, "Do you know who the patient is?"

"I don't know his name . . . an accident on the Haute Corniche." The orderly thumped his chest with his hand to illustrate the injuries.

"Can you tell me about the girl? The one who was admitted this afternoon."

The orderly said, "The girl? There were two girls. . . ."

"An American girl . . . Marion Sargesson. She's seventeen."

"*Ah, oui* . . . the American girl." The porter nodded his head.

Sargesson had to make a conscious effort to steady his voice. "Do you know where she is now?"

"*Ah, oui,* she's in there . . . the room at the end." The orderly was pointing back toward the entrance. Sargesson walked back toward the lateral doors, knowing now that everything *was* okay. The door on the right was slightly ajar and it was dark beyond. He looked back at the orderly, who nodded vigorously.

He stepped in. He said quietly, "Honey?"

From the acoustics he knew the place was big, maybe a reserve operating room. She didn't answer. As his eyes grew accustomed to the semidarkness he realized that he was in some sort of lecture room. The tiers of chairs fell away below him. Then he saw the gurney only a pace away from him to his right.

"Marion," he whispered. But even as he said it he realized that she must be asleep. With his left hand he reached back to open the door wide and the beam of light spread and fell across her.

From long experience he knew she was dead.

He stood there motionless for fully five minutes staring down at her face, which still had the luster of life. It was smooth and unhurt and her lips were set in the familiar half-obstinate expression. He couldn't move, couldn't think, couldn't realize she had gone. Once he reached out to touch the small sickle scar on her temple where she had slipped on the rocks at Cape Cod. Her skin was soft and cool, and he left his finger there a minute, hoping for God knew what.

He never heard them come. The lights went on blindingly and two men in overalls went to either end of the gurney.

"M'sieu," one of them said, and crossed himself.

Then they were swinging and moving it back into the hall. He walked slowly into the doorway after them. They pushed her stolidly away through the electronic doors and along the covered walk. There were sounds behind him, and when he turned he saw the team coming out of the operating room and going into the room next door.

A surgeon still in his operating clothes was talking to the orderly. His mask was pulled down and he had a hard young face behind horn-rimmed spectacles. A moment later he was padding down in his sterilized boots.

"Doctor Sargesson? Is that right?"

His muscular hand gripped Sargesson's own. "I'm sorry . . . really very sorry. One minute . . ."

He walked back and the orderly gave him a cigarette. He waited, hunched while the orderly lit it for him, and then he returned to Sargesson. He had the Italianate face of the region, and when he came back it was set in solemn introspection, a look that was as formalized as the surgical mask. Sargesson recognized an expression that he used himself.

Vallier said, "Let's go into the garden. . . ."

They walked out through the electronic doors and turned a corner away from the covered walk onto a terrace contained by flowering shrubs and a low hedge. On a lower terrace, chair patients were grouped in the late sunshine, and a few young nurses had already started taking them back to the main building.

"I sunbathe here often when I am waiting. What did they tell you?"

"I just had a message to say my daughter had been admitted. I came over right away. I saw her there. . . ."

"They haven't spoken to you? Is that right?"

"No. Nobody's told me anything."

Vallier hit his forehead lightly with his open palm. *"Merde!"*

He drew deeply on his cigarette and went to lean against an old olive tree that had survived among the shrubs. Again Sargesson recognized a pattern of behavior and knew that Vallier was giving himself time to think.

Vallier said, "You know your daughter had been pregnant. That is right?"

Sargesson turned away. "No, I . . . I didn't know that." In the quietness, the sound of voices from the terrace below was audible. One of the nurses was laughing breathlessly as she moved a patient to the ramp.

"She was . . . was *avortée*." By using the French word Vallier had maybe hoped to make it sound less brutal.

Sargesson couldn't speak. The shock was not only in the news itself, but that she had never told him, never asked his advice. Vallier went on talking but it was several seconds before Sargesson turned his mind back to the soft voice. ". . . brought in from some motel below Eze. I'd already put out a call for the anesthetist and the operating room staff after they had telephoned. When they brought her in, her pulse rate was rapid and the pulse was thin. She was pale, you know . . . and I immediately started an intravenous infusion with a vasopressor and took some blood for typing and matching. As soon as the blood arrived I started her on it." Vallier shook his head. He looked very tired. "I asked the ambulance driver whether there had been much blood lost there or in the ambulance . . . they are trained to observe these things, but he'd been in too much of a hurry. . . ."

A moment later he slid his back down the tree and stayed there. He stubbed out his cigarette. "There was too much blood gone, but I pumped in more quickly. Her pulse rate came down and her blood pressure was up to a systolic of nearly a hundred. I thought there was a chance." He stopped suddenly.

His hands were spread in the Kikuyu grass which grew like a cushion under the tree. He looked up at Sargesson for the second time. His heavy-lidded quattrocento face seemed to be even more tired suddenly. "You want me to tell you everything? Is that right?"

Sargesson moved to the low hedge. The terrace below

was empty now. Farther down the valley two water sprays crossed and recrossed above a vineyard. He went back to the weary man under the tree. "Yes, I want to hear it all."

Vallier sighed and his voice sank to a mumble, and Sargesson had to stand right over him to hear. "By now Cremoux had arrived. He considered it safe to give her anesthesia for a D and C."

"D and E," Sargesson said abruptly. "Evacuation, not curettage."

"D and E, yes, of course," Vallier whispered, his voice even quieter. "He gave her a light general anesthetic and kept pumping in blood. I started to operate. The cervix was wide open. I took away the clot and . . . and debris from the body of the uterus. We continued the transfusion and gave her Ergometrine and then still more. It was no good. The uterus remained flabby and wouldn't respond. And the bleeding wouldn't stop either. . . .

"Cremoux told me that the blood pressure was dropping again. I decided to pack the uterus. Frequently, as you know, it will save a life. But the bleeding continued . . . dark and red . . ." Vallier's eyes closed. "Cremoux had her on a hundred percent oxygen and the vasopressor. It was still no good. Soon the pulse went . . . and the blood pressure . . . at the end not even cardiac massage helped her. . . ."

Vallier shook his head angrily. "The bleeding should have stopped when all the tissue had gone but it was dripping into my boots. Nothing else to do . . . what *else* can you do for neurogenic shock except give her intravenous cortisone, which we did. It was the shock that killed her . . . the shock. *Ces . . . ces bouchers!*" His hands curled into fists.

A helicopter swept over their heads, following the coastline into the darkening east. As the sound of the rotors faded, Vallier stood up and stamped his feet. "I must tell them where I am. . . ." He moved away, walking slowly.

Sargesson, walking a pace behind, heard him say, "I've got some cognac in the laboratory."

"Another time maybe." They walked back through the electronic doors into the surgery wing. Sargesson held out his hand. "Thank you for everything you did."

Vallier shrugged and shook his hand. "I'm sorry," he said.

Sargesson walked back to the main building and found his way to the reception hall. One of the girls there sent to Casualty for Marion's personal belongings while he called the hospital in Villefranche and arranged for her to be collected and taken to the morgue. They brought her things in a paper bag, and he signed the receipt and went out into the scented evening.

Gauron must have been watching for him, because the car rolled forward as soon as he appeared at the top of the steps. He went down and entered the rear door, putting the paper bag on the seat beside him. There was a patch of blood on the corner of it, he noticed, already congealed.

After they'd come down the avénue Leopold from the Corniche and were waiting at the traffic lights, Gauron turned his head to say, "Shall I take you straight home, Doctor?"

"No, I don't think so. I'll go back to the hospital."

And when they got there he directed Gauron to the parking lot and got straight into his own car and drove home. After he'd withdrawn his key and closed the front door, he stayed with his head touching the cool mahogany panel. Realization seemed to come with that final act of closing the door, as if it were the last item of data in a computer program.

The reaction began immediately, but not in any overt way. The frigidity of his nature and the professional discipline of years would still not allow him to trust himself to any emotion. His pain showed in his open-eyed stillness, the total immobility of a hurt animal. He stood there an hour before the coma passed. Then he picked up the paper bag at his feet and went into her room.

She had hurriedly half-made her bed before she left, shaking up her quilt and straightening the pillows, but the place was as untidy as ever. He opened the bag on her desk and lifted out her things. Then he crossed and recrossed the room methodically, putting them away in the same way he might have done if she'd just come back from a holiday or a weekend with her cousin in Paris. He hung her crumpled dress in the wardrobe and put her shoes on the rack. There were no tights, only her bra and the bloodstained panties, and he walked through into the bathroom and dropped them into the clothes hamper as if she really would be needing them again.

Her personal belongings had been put separately in a

plastic envelope, and he shook them out loosely on the desk. The head scarf he put in the top drawer of the chest. Then he picked up her accessories one by one— the half-dozen narrow bracelets she always wore, and the small lapis lazuli ring, the replica of a butterfly, which she had bought in the flea market in Nice only a few months ago.

And the locket.

Of all her possessions the locket was the thing they both treasured most. It was an old sovereign case in dark gold, which his mother had always worn. His wife had worn it briefly, too, but hadn't bothered to take it when she left. He put the bracelets and the ring in the casket on her dresser with her other jewelry, most of which, with a lot of Tiffany glass, she had inherited from his sister. The locket he put in his pocket. He kept his hand clasped around it as if it were some kind of talisman.

Only her handbag was left. It was Moroccan, of embossed leather, with a shoulder strap. When he opened it, it looked as it always did—like a magpie's nest. He stood for a moment before carrying it into the living room. He opened the french windows onto the balcony before going to the sideboard and setting out bottles. He made himself a gimlet, lifting the measure to eye level and mixing it as carefully as a prescription. He stirred it without ice and poured half of it into a wineglass before taking it to the corner desk.

He opened her handbag there, sorting everything methodically again. There must have been fifty coins, francs and centimes, and he set them out in piles. Then there were her cosmetics, a tube of blusher, a couple of lipsticks and a box of eyeshadow. In a pocket he found a fold of ten-franc notes and a card for her dental appointment at the end of the week with Douglas Walter.

In another pocket he found old bus tickets and an appointment book. He held the book under the light, flipping the pages quickly. It had been kept industriously for the first three months of the year and then had petered out. Nothing had been written in since a month back, not even the dental appointment. In the biggest compartment of the bag there was a flat packet of tissues and a well-worn paperback edition of Henry James's *Wings of the Dove*, which she was reading for her literature exams. He leafed through it while he sipped his drink. Passages were underlined in several colors, and occasional exclamation marks leaped at him from the margin. He put it aside at last and rummaged in the empty bag. What at first he thought was stiffening in the bottom turned out to be another zip-up pocket. He opened the zip and withdrew a small oblong notebook and a photograph with broken corners. The photograph was of his wife, one taken when they were vacationing on Cape Cod, and he automatically tore it into small pieces, which he carried out to the wastebasket in the kitchen. Then he came back and opened the notebook — "Marion Sargesson, Her Diary," it said on the opening page, and thereafter every day's page was crammed with small neat handwriting, right up until the day she died.

He fell asleep in his chair. It was cold and some time

after midnight when he woke and stumbled into the bedroom and undressed. He left the door and window open as usual. Lying there watching the window curtains billowing in the draft of air, he called softly, "Good night, Fizz. . . . Good night, honey. . . ." And after several minutes, while he hoped for God knew what miracle to happen, he whispered, "Wherever you are."

Eventually in the empty darkness he fell asleep.

10

IT WAS HALF AN HOUR SINCE HE HAD HEARD THE LAST
distant thunderclap, and now there was only the sound
of a gutter dripping outside like the beat of a funeral
drum.

The shaker was empty and the record had finished a
quarter-hour ago, and he knew he was consciously de-
laying the moment when the routine of the evening
would begin. Looking across at the pale figure in the
chaise he knew it was because *she* was there tonight.
Already her presence seemed anthropomorphic.

He stood up suddenly and went out into the passage
and along to the cellar door. He unlocked it with a key
from his key case and propped it open with the brick he
kept there on the top step. When he went back to pick
her up, her hair swung realistically across her face. He
carried her along and propped her against the wall by
the door. Then he went into the kitchen for the rest of
her things. He piled the pump and the wardrobe carton
beside her.

He went out through the kitchen to the old pantry off the back passage. Since Peyrouse had called on him in August, he had kept the formaldehyde there, and he now poured a cupful into a clean plastic bucket and added water from the faucet over the sink. He fitted an airtight lid to the bucket and picked up another empty bucket before taking them both through. At the head of the cellar steps he switched on a light and picked up the leaning figure and went on down.

The hallway was painted white now and there was a trestle table on the side opposite the steel door, which was stacked with most of the things he needed from day to day. Also, the blast walls were gone and the door to the first chamber sealed up. Access to it was now only through the communicating door from the second chamber. He put the figure down against the table and lowered the buckets. Then he picked up the periscope which he had made by fixing a sort of large version of a dental mirror to a length of rod. Beside the steel door, at eye height, there was a wooden plug fixed to an iron strip, which was held by latches on either side. He raised the bar and withdrew the plug and pushed the mirror through, twisting it to reflect the room beyond.

Kemp was sitting on the iron bed reading. As he withdrew the mirror, Kemp must have seen the movement, because Sargesson heard the bedsprings jangle and Kemp's distant Lilliputian shouting.

"You're late again! You're always bloody late. And don't tell me my watch is wrong because I know! My bloody guts told me! And my biological time clock . . ."

Sargesson slipped the wooden plug back into the hole, muffling the voice. Then he bent down and opened the steel door by spinning a wheel gear which moved the bolts in and out of their sockets. It opened soundlessly, and he went into the antechamber. A second steel door into Kemp's dormitory room was also controlled by a wheel mechanism in the passage.

There were kitchen units at one end of the antechamber and a ventilator fan which fed into an old chimney above. On the wall to his left was the exercise bicycle and the sunlamp and a few other things that Kemp was allowed during his occupational periods. Everything was laid out neatly and every item of kitchen equipment hung from a low-level hook so that he could check everything instantly when Kemp was back in his cell. He went out for the buckets and brought them in, putting the empty one under the drainpipe of the stainless steel sink.

Sargesson opened the wall refrigerator and checked the contents. There were butter and fruit juice there, a few cold potatoes and half an apple pie, which Kemp had baked from last week's pastry mix. He closed the refrigerator, and as he was going back to the passage again he saw Kemp's fingertips through the observation grille set into the top half of the cell door and the segmented shape of Kemp's face above. But Kemp didn't speak, and Sargesson went on by to fetch the pump and the rest of the gear and put it into the antechamber. Then he went up to the kitchen to get Kemp's food rations, which he stacked neatly into a carton. He took it down to the cellar, and this time he removed the brick and closed the door at the top of the steps behind him.

He put the carton of food on the kitchen table, then went to the inspection grille in Kemp's door. Kemp was now standing in the middle of the room.

His thumbs were hooked in the belt of his jeans and he looked calmly back at Sargesson. "What is the time anyway . . ."

"Twenty-five after seven."

Kemp moved away restlessly out of his field of vision and when he came back he was farther from the grille. Without interest he said, "What's for dinner?"

"Oh, some of those mutton chops you said you liked last week."

"I *didn't* say I liked them."

"You did, Kemp. Don't you remember? It was when I . . ."

"You're a lying bastard!"

Sargesson didn't reply, and the silence that followed was total. He had often noticed it before. There were no extraneous sounds, only the sound of breathing, or feet scraping, or the whisper of fabric when someone moved.

At last Sargesson said, "As a matter of fact, I've got a surprise for you tonight. I don't know whether you'll like it. It's kind of problematic, but I thought I'd give it a try."

"What is it? What have you got?"

"It's okay. You'll see in a minute."

Kemp had come right up to the grille again, and his tanned face was pressed against it as he tried to see the space on either side of the door. Then he said wearily, "It's not another *game*, is it? Like those goddam solitaire skittles . . ."

"I try to make things easy for you, Kemp. I thought they might amuse you."

"Oh, for Christ's sake . . ."

Sargesson moved away out into the passageway. He pulled the heavy door closed behind him. As he started spinning the wheel lock he said, "It's seven-thirty, Kemp. You have until nine-thirty as usual."

Then he spun the lower wheel in the opposite direction to open the door of Kemp's cell. Although he must have heard the bolts being drawn, it was a long time before Kemp emerged. Sargesson, watching, waited impatiently.

When Kemp finally came out he turned right and walked straight down the center of the cell to the kitchen table. He put down the lavatory bucket he was carrying and switched on the sunlamp and the ventilator fan over the cooker. He started to unpack the food from the carton.

Sargesson, waiting, knew that Kemp's behavior was deliberate. It had happened before whenever he had tried to introduce some improvement in Kemp's living conditions. It was Kemp's way of denying his dependence on Sargesson. It was about five minutes before Kemp turned, and then he stood for a moment staring at the girl's figure with a look of utter incredulity. The next moment he was bent double with ostentatious laughter. It went on, forced and harsh, for fully a minute before he walked unsteadily down to the door panel.

"You're fucking crazy, Sargesson! You have to believe it now!"

Sargesson stepped quickly away from the panel and back against the wall. Let Kemp think he had gone.

"Sargesson!" His shout rang like a sustained note in the passageway. "Sargesson, you shit!"

Then in a lowered voice Kemp said, "I know you're there." He sighed deeply. "And if you were hoping for a bit of voyeurism you can piss off."

Sargesson saw the blunt ends of Kemp's fingers suddenly sprout through the grille. "Know you're there," Kemp said in a childish singsong voice. "Know you're there! Know you're there! Know you're there!" Then there was silence. The fingers were withdrawn.

Sargesson was considering moving back to the grille when Kemp began to speak in a clear, serious voice. "I am not a fucking domestic pet, Sargesson. You cannot reduce me to *that*. I am not a fucking parakeet with an exercise wheel and a food dispenser and another little plastic parakeet for company."

Suddenly Sargesson could stand it no longer. In two strides he was back at the grille. "Shut up!" he shouted. "Shut up!"

He had not been so angry in a long time. He saw Kemp's shocked face turned toward him. "Just listen to me, Kemp," he said in a voice that still shook. "I went to considerable risk to buy this thing. I had to spend nearly half an hour in one of those fuck shops off Victor Hugo. You might say I put my professional reputation on the line for you because if anyone had seen me . . ."

He turned away from the grille and closed his mouth abruptly. He was angry now with himself. Why did it always end this way, with shouting and abuse? The same thing had happened when he had brought the sunlamp and the bicycle. Kemp's isolation had somehow made him incapable of rational understanding.

He moved closer to the grille again. He said patiently, "You've always been a womanizer, Kemp. I can't provide you with a real woman, so all I can do is try to take care of your sexual deprivation. I thought . . ."

"Well, you thought bloody well wrong."

"It's better than masturbating, Kemp," he said primly. "Don't forget, I have to attend to your laundry myself."

There were tears on Kemp's cheeks suddenly. It was one of those damn days. But they were tears of frustration. Kemp said, very slowly, "I don't want to fuck a plastic imitation . . . *that* is obscene . . . an obscene perversion. Don't you see that? Masturbation is what's normal in this hellish situation. Don't you realize that? Oh, Christ . . ." Kemp brushed a hand across his face and they stared at each other through the grille. There was a wall to their understanding as thick and as impenetrable as the prison wall.

"As I told you, Kemp, I went to considerable trouble. I only meant it for the best." Sargesson turned away.

He would leave it there, though, the way he'd left the other things. Kemp would see he was right in the end. "I'll be back at nine-thirty."

He walked away, up the concrete passage, with his hands hung out characteristically. Sometimes he returned silently to watch Kemp prepare his meal or pedal away under the sunlamp, but it had been a day of great strain and he went straight to the kitchen to fix his own dinner.

He put on water for the rice and heated up some of the curry mixture he kept in the refrigerator. While he waited he gathered up the cartons and the packing and carried them into the back pantry. At the weekend he would burn them in the garden incinerator. He was stacking them on a slatted shelf when a folded green card drifted to the floor between his feet.

He picked it up. It was printed in four languages under a bouquet of national flags. The English version read:

"My name is Kiki.

Please . . . wash me only in warm water and mild detergent

. . . lubricate me only with the cosmetic oils supplied by the manufacturer

. . . when you don't need me always store me in a dry place

Thank you very much."

The warranty card was printed beneath and stated that the Ingerschraft Novelty Company of Amsterdam would replace any defective item if it was notified within one month of purchase.

Sargesson turned the card over.

"Je m'appelle Kiki.
S'il vous plaît . . ."

He tore it in half and dropped it back into the empty
carton.

PART II

1

ON THE FIRST DAY OF HIS VACATION KEMP HAD PLANNED an early start.

He'd loaded the Bentley up the night before with his diving gear and a pile of books he intended to read and he hoped to drive clear down the *autostrada* in two days and take the ferry across to Sicily. Everything would depend on the traffic density, but once he was clear of the Riviera he anticipated no problem.

It was the beginning of September, when most of Europe was going back to work and the Mediterranean would still be warm. A year ago diving there, just off Syracuse, he had discovered half a dozen amphorae, two of which were in perfect condition, and also a piece of hewn timber which looked just about as old. He had the feeling he might have been near to finding some ancient wreck, so he was going back.

He took the elevator down to the parking lot for the last time, loaded with potted plants which Madame Harel, the concierge, was going to look after for him.

He spread a newspaper on the table outside her door before putting them down.

It was just before seven, and the morning was pale rose when he started up the Bentley and swept powerfully down through the shadow of the plane trees toward the coast. He was checking the instruments on the dash and slowing down for the turn into the avénue Maréchal Foch when a wild-looking figure broke from the shadow of a tree and stood waving on the side of the road.

As he braked sharply he recognized Sargesson. "Hi, Sarge . . . what the hell are you doing here?" When he pushed up his goggles he saw that Sargesson was looking pale and shaken.

Sargesson said, "Oh, Peter . . . thank God I caught you." He leaned on the side of the open cockpit.

"What's wrong?"

Sargesson wiped his face briefly with a hand. "I have a problem . . . could I hitch a ride with you? Can you take me home? Bellegarde's on your way, isn't it?"

"Okay." Kemp was a little irritated all the same. It was bound to mean a bit of a delay. Sargesson climbed in awkwardly and sat like a bundle of sticks with his slim medical case across his knees.

Kemp said, "What happened?"

"I'll explain as we go."

As Kemp sped on down to the lower Corniche Sargesson twisted sideways to speak close to his ear. "I was on call and they got me in about five-thirty for a Mrs. Herkel . . ."

"I know. Rich widow."

"That's right." And Sargesson added, "All she

needed was an emetic. Then on the way back I hit some kind of oil patch and ran under the back of this truck. It wasn't too serious, but the steering jammed. A couple of men helped me push it into a gas station. Then I tried to call up the hospital and a cab, but the pay phone was out of order. Then I remembered that you lived just around the corner."

"I'll run you back to the hospital if you like."

"No, I think I'll get home. I'll call them from there and get them to take care of the car."

They reached the end of the boulevard, and Kemp turned left into the early morning traffic stream along the Corniche Inférieure. The Mediterranean was slate blue, and a flock of gray-backed gulls were diving on a patch of flotsam in the new yacht marina at Beaulieu. The Bentley flashed into the outer lane and passed a convoy of French army transports. Kemp noticed that Sargesson was bent away to the other side and was wiping his face with a handkerchief.

He said, "Sure you're okay, Sarge?"

"I'm fine." Sargesson finished wiping his face with care and folded the handkerchief before putting it away in his breast pocket. "Sorry to give you this trouble."

"No trouble. Glad to be of help."

"I may as well tell you I wouldn't normally have called up at your place, but I've had this virus for a couple of days, the same thing that's going around the staff wing, I guess."

"You should have taken yourself off duty." They were going faster now, and Kemp had to shout against the slipstream.

"Couldn't do that," Sargesson shouted back. "Lavaud's away and your trip was coming up. Just get me home. I'll be all right."

When they reached Bellegarde-Plage Sargesson directed him to the loop road up the hill. The sea was paler and more choppy against the west side of the promontory. At the lower speed talking was easier. Kemp said, "This is some occasion, isn't it? I'll be the first one to see this hidey-hole of yours."

"Well . . . it *is* out of the way. These days when I'm not on duty or standby or anything I prefer to get away from it all."

Kemp drove in silence for half a mile before he said, "You really think that's such a good idea, Sarge? I mean . . . don't you think . . ."

"I could hardly stay on after Marion died. You must see that." Sargesson sounded like his old-maidish self again.

"I only mean that it's a long way from work and friends."

"It has other advantages, as you will see."

"I'm sure it has, and I'm pleased to be the first one to see it. Everyone's been very curious." They drove in silence, swaying together with the twists in the loop road, until at last the viaduct was above them, somber against the morning sky.

"That's the viaduct. The British tried to bomb it during the war, you know. Several times. It was the rail link with the Italian front . . . this and the Anthéor viaduct were the principal targets for their strategic bombing on this bit of the coast." Kemp didn't know and he wasn't all that interested. The war was a long time gone. Sargesson directed him up the long spur under the shadow of a château. Then they rose farther through cobbled streets and eventually came to the trim villas of a housing development.

Kemp said politely, "Looks great."

"Oh, it's not one of these ... it's got a lot more character."

They entered the final cul-de-sac, and Kemp slowed down. Sargesson said, "We won't use the driveway, if you don't mind, as it hasn't been properly finished yet. You can turn and park here." Then he took the handkerchief from his breast pocket again.

"Sarge?" Kemp snapped on the hand brake and looked at him.

"I'm ... I'm okay. Just this bloody infection."

Kemp said firmly, "You need a couple of shots and into bed."

"I hope you'll join me. You've been a great help. I was shaken up more than I thought."

"Well ... a quick one for the road, maybe," Kemp said reluctantly.

As he climbed out Sargesson was ahead of Kemp, opening the new iron gate. They walked up the silent driveway, skirting puddles here and there. The only sound was something rattling in Sargesson's medical bag and a murmur of aspen leaves.

Kemp said, "How old is it? Did you have to do much to it?"

"Not a hell of a lot. A few minor structural improvements," Sargesson said calmly. "You'll find it pretty interesting in some ways. There it is."

They came out into the clearing in front of the house, and shafts of early sunlight through the trees were spotlighting the roof gables. Kemp said with surprise, "Why, Sarge, it's great. Old-fashioned in just the right kind of way. Do you have much land?"

"About an acre . . . and there's the barn behind."

They walked on up the driveway to the steps, and while Sargesson put down his bag and got out his key case Kemp swung away to look at the garden. He called from a distance, "It's really secluded . . . you could do just about anything you wanted here."

Sargesson smiled slightly while he waited until Kemp came up the steps, then led the way in.

Behind him Kemp said, "It really must be a quickie, Sarge. I've got a hell of a drive."

"I understand. Is Scotch okay? I *could* make coffee. . . ."

"No, Scotch is fine." And Kemp added, without conviction, "You're real cozy."

"Well, it's the way I found it, but it kind of appeals to me. I'll get some ice."

After he'd gone Kemp prowled around the bookshelves. Sargesson, someone, had picked a lot of roses, three or four bowls of them, and their scent filled the room. When he came to the stereo, he looked down at the old records lying there. He muttered, "Oh boy," in a desperate kind of way.

Sargesson came back and gave him a glass. "It's not the greatest Scotch in the world but it was all they had at the supermarket." And he added, almost with petulance, "Sit down."

"Well . . . okay. Besides, there's something I must say to you, Sarge. I tried to say it in the car. . . ."

"What's that?"

"I'm worried about you. We're all worried about you — Josh, Fran, Ralph, the whole bunch." He drank half of his whiskey, and almost grimaced. Sarge had been right. It was bloody awful Scotch.

"Why should they be worried about me?"

"Well, it's the way you've cut yourself off. And when I tell them about this gloomy place . . ."

"But I don't find it gloomy."

"When *did* you last have a holiday?"

"Me? Oh, I don't know. . . . Marion and I used to go to Spain, you know."

"Yes, I remember she talked about it."

"The wrong side of Marbella, some people would call it, a little town called San Pedro. The market was very, very beautiful, and an American general and his wife ran a paperback book library there. We didn't do a great deal except swim and comb the beaches. Let me freshen that drink for you?"

Kemp shielded his glass involuntarily. "No, it's fine, really." He watched Sargesson turning away and adding an inch to his own glass.

"You're the first guest I've had." And he added, feebly, "I suppose you could call it a housewarming."

Kemp yawned. "It's having a soporific effect. . . . I must be more tired than I thought."

Sargesson straightened a framed portrait of Marion that was on the cocktail cabinet and moved away, walking behind Kemp's chair. "I think Marion *would* have liked it here, you know. She always wanted some place big enough to keep a horse. . . . This would have been fine for that. She often went riding at those stables back of Villefranche. There's hardly anywhere to go except up and down the same hill. I was going to buy her a young mare for her eighteenth birthday . . . that would have been next month." He stopped at the long window which the first full blaze of the sun was just reaching. "She was always very fond of everything outdoors. She was kind of like you in that respect, wasn't she? You're always skiing or diving or something. . . ."

Sargesson's figure was outlined against the brilliant window, and Kemp found it a strain to look at him. He closed his eyes and said, "Sarge, there's something else I ought to tell you. . . ."

"What's that?"

"It's about Marion." The room seemed stiller than before, so that the song of a blackbird over by the barn was piercingly sweet. With a rush, Kemp said, "It's what we all feel, really . . . you know . . . that maybe you let the thing prey on your mind a bit. You know how these things can go as well as I do. She's been dead a good while now . . . it must be around seven months, isn't it? And . . ." He opened his eyes with an effort and saw that Sargesson had moved away from the window glare and was standing at the mantelpiece.

Turning, Sargesson said, "Six months, if you want to get it right. Six months, eleven days, and, oh . . . around fifteen hours."

"That's what I mean," said Kemp, and was surprised that his speech was slurred. "Keeping on . . ."

Sargesson came down to stand over him, suddenly.

In a snapping voice he said, "I'm surprised she doesn't prey on other people's minds."

"I don't know what you mean by that," Kemp said wearily, and closed his eyes again. "We all remember her, of course . . ."

"You know how she died, don't you?" Sargesson was sounding a little unbalanced, and Kemp knew it was time to go. As he emptied his glass Sargesson was saying, "Well, don't you think she'd prey on the mind of the man responsible for her death?"

"You must stop thinking about it, Sarge . . . talking like this. . . . Believe me . . ."

"You're right," Sargesson said suddenly, and again there seemed to be an extra stillness in the room. A petal falling from one of the roses would have been audible. He said, "Let's drink to her memory, and then I shan't mention her again."

Kemp moved to the edge of his chair and swayed. "Christ, that really hit me. . . ." He put his glass down, looking surprised. "Sarge? . . ." He was vaguely aware of a clicking sound and then a moment later a light kind of voice was singing.

He sat back in the chair, feeling a wave of dizziness. He said thickly, "Sarge . . . I think . . . water . . ." With a great effort he opened his eyes, screwing them into focus.

Sargesson was carrying a banner . . . no, not a banner. It was a cloak, he thought, and Sargesson was holding it out to one side like a bullfighter's cape. In his last moments of consciousness Kemp was just able to see the canvas straps and buckles of a straitjacket.

And then, like a dying bull, he struggled to his feet

and went forward in a blind, stumbling rush. A tripod table rolled with his fall and the cheap gilded bowl on it cracked neatly in half. Kemp lay with his face half turned up and roses scattered at his waist.

The tinny voice drowned the sound of his heavy breathing.

"Isn't this a lovely day to be caught in the rain? You Were going on your way now you've got to remain. Just as you were going . . ."

WHEN KEMP OPENED HIS EYES FOR THE FIRST TIME HE SAW only the plastic bottle and the tube above his head.

The second impression he had was one of restraint and he closed his eyes again. He knew immediately that a recurring nightmare had come true. . . . He'd failed to hold the Bentley on a bend or else one of those big trailer trucks had swung out and chopped him. Whatever had happened, here he was strapped up in a casualty ward.

His head ached.

He tried to remember the drive. How far had he got when it happened? But nothing came back to him, and he suspected that spinal or head injuries were bound to have concussed him. The Bentley was a bloody great thing to crash, nearly a ton and a half.

He strained to remember.

He knew he'd started out, because he could remember stacking his gear on top of the folded down rear seat and strapping it in. Then, locking the apartment and carrying the plants down to Madame Harel.

Sargesson. He'd met Sargesson on the road. . . .

He opened his eyes again and turned his head. He was in a concrete cell. Then, looking down, he saw the straitjacket. He moved violently against the restriction, but found that his legs were bound. He could just raise his head high enough to see the heavy-duty medical tape that wrapped them to the iron frame of the bed on either side.

He said, "Christ!" loudly.

Up till then he had felt almost relieved, that whatever was going on he hadn't been crushed under the Bentley. That drink with Sargesson, the straitjacket . . . Sargesson, he realized now, was playing some stupid, fucking game. He had always thought he was a nut, and Marion's death must have finally sent him round the bend.

"Sarge?" His voice shook slightly.

Louder, he said, "Sarge? For Christ's sake . . . what's going on?"

The silence remained total. Not even air stirred. "Sarge! Sarge! Sarge!" he shouted at the top of his voice, but the name was drowned in the double echo. He raised his head again. From waist to knee he was wrapped in a huge bath towel. Farther up there was more tape across the straitjacket, so that he could in fact move only his head. He looked down at the towel again and had a sudden irrational fear that he had been castrated. If Sargesson was crazy he was capable of anything.

"Sargesson!"

He waited half a minute then yelled again. "Sargesson, you bloody maniac!"

The door of the cell was visible beyond the end of the bed and there was an observation panel of latticed steel set into the top half of it. He closed his eyes. Maybe he really *had* gone crazy, he thought for a second, but immediately rejected the idea. He looked up again at the plastic bottle and the tube swinging down beside his head. There was liquid in the bottle held, he supposed, by a draw valve and it was there for him to drink.

He moved his head sideways until he could grip the tube in his teeth. He sucked for a moment and then tasted the sweetness of glucose in his mouth. Maybe there was a sedative mixed up in the glucose, because soon afterward he fell asleep again.

When he woke for the second time his legs ached and he badly wanted to piss. "Sarge!" he yelled again and kept yelling for half a minute. "Sarge! I know you're there!"

There was still no sound and he decided to piss anyway. He felt the heat of the urine slowly spread through the bath towel against his skin. He realized then that that was what the towel was for. And the glucose was to keep him going. Sargesson would be at the hospital, of course. But what the fucking hell was it all about? What was going on? Where was he?

In the basement of that stupid Gothic house that Sargesson had bought? For the first time he felt a twitch of fright. Why should Sargesson have gone to all this trouble? For what reason? After a while he dozed again.

He didn't know how long he lay there, though he realized later it must have been about two days. He just dozed, shouted occasionally, and dozed again. Eventually the bottle was empty and his urine had stained the towel yellow. He never heard Sargesson come back.

He never heard the door open, or anything else. He just opened his eyes and saw Sargesson standing at the foot of the bed, watching him with the same clinical detachment as he must have watched patients.

In a voice that shook slightly he said, "Sarge, let me out of this bloody thing!"

Sargesson continued to watch him without speaking. Then he went to the head of the bed and unhooked the bottle and tube and carried them through the door to whatever was beyond. As he came back, Kemp said, "If this is some stupid joke . . ."

"It isn't a joke, Kemp."

"Well, what do you fucking think you're doing?" Kemp was almost screaming. "Let me out of this!"

Sargesson said primly, "I'll let you out in a moment."

Kemp sighed. "Well, thank Christ for that." He turned his head and said savagely, "You might just tell me what it's all about. . . ."

"Certainly. It's all quite simple." He went out to the other place again and came back carrying a bucket with a lid. "This is your slop bucket, which you can keep in here with you."

"Look, just undo me." Kemp's eyes were hot with

tears of frustration. "You said you were letting me out.
. . . Sarge!"

"There's a stove and a sink in the other room, Kemp,
and there's food and most of the other things you'll
need. I've brought your books in from the car, by the
way. You'll be allowed in there for two hours every
night to prepare food and wash yourself and so on.
From around seven-thirty to nine-thirty, after I'm back
from the hospital. . . ."

"Listen to me, Sarge." Kemp spoke with all the authority and patience he had. "If you stop and think for
a moment, it must be pretty obvious you've had some
kind of breakdown. Now, there's no real harm done yet.
You need help . . . whatever the problem is, I'm sure
Josh Weiss can straighten it out. I'll go along with
you."

"There's also a transistor radio in there, which you
can keep with you. This place is completely soundproof, by the way, so play it as loud as you like."

"It's about Marion, isn't it, Sarge? She's . . . preyed
on your mind."

"As she should have preyed on yours."

"I don't know what you mean."

"She was in love with you, a fact of which you took
advantage. And when she became pregnant you aborted
her. You were her lover and her murderer."

"This is really crazy talk! I don't know where you
heard it, Sarge, but I can tell you here and now that it is
a load of shit. I liked Marion very much. She was a
good friend."

And as Sargesson stood there unmoved, he shouted,

"If this whole charade is because you think *that,* then you're making a really terrible mistake! Sarge, listen to me. . . ." His voice lowered again. "I had nothing to do with her death. You can't do this to me, it's . . . fucking insane!"

"Not insane. The situation is quite rational, if you think about it." Sargesson turned away and went to the door. Then he said, "It's no good, Kemp, is it? I know when and where you made love. . . . She visited you up in your apartment. . . ."

"Never," shouted Kemp.

"And you actually met her at *my* house, on a day when I was doing your duty for you and you were supposed to be at a meeting of the Villefranche Ski Club. But you weren't, were you? . . ."

Kemp shook his head wearily.

"Wait a minute now, Sarge . . . just wait a minute. I don't know how you got it wrong, but I know we can sort it out. You were right about the Ski Club but I wasn't with Marion; I was with a new chick and we drove to San Remo."

"And Marion didn't visit you at your apartment?"

"No . . . never. Whoever told you that was way out."

"Were they? I don't think so."

"Well, whoever it is, it's certainly his word against mine and I have . . ."

"Her word." Sargesson said it quietly. "You see, it was Marion told me."

As the total silence came back Kemp seemed to sink into the bed. He closed his eyes and whispered, "Oh Jesus . . ." Sargesson moved up to the side of the bed and took some surgical scissors from his pocket.

Kemp whispered, "But why should she *do* that! What was her motive in telling you a *lie.*"

"Oh, give it up, Kemp. Your address was in her diary. She was there three or four days before she died."

"Oh Christ, now I remember. They . . . they had a meeting there, she and some other kids. . . ."

"It's no good, I have all the evidence in writing." Sargesson bent and cut the tapes that bound Kemp's chest to the bed.

Suddenly, before he could straighten, Kemp's body had jackknifed and Kemp's head had smashed into his own.

He fell sideways beside the bed with blood streaming from his nose. As he saw Kemp twist desperately down toward him, snarling like a dog, he rolled away out of reach. Still held by the ankles, Kemp was jerking and flailing with his whole body, but the iron legs of the bed had been sunk deep into the reinforced concrete and didn't move. Sargesson had sunk them himself, with the cement and sand the builder had left him. After a moment Kemp lay back, straining for breath in long, harsh gasps. Sargesson climbed slowly to his feet, searched for and found the scissors. He kept a handkerchief to his nose, pinching the nostril in which the rupture had occurred, in his usual way.

As he went toward the door Kemp was shouting at him hysterically. "She would never have told you, Sargesson! She would have told anyone else before she told a moralizing iceberg like you. . . ."

Sargesson stopped at the door and turned. His voice

was muffled but quite audible. "Oh, I know that, Kemp," he said. "She didn't tell me verbally. I found her diary, you see, after she was dead. It even itemized the occasions on which you made love to her."

"Well, it was *lies*, Sargesson, all lies! For whatever reason. . . ."

Sargesson went out and the door closed. After a short pause Kemp heard the tumblers fall and the bolts creaking home.

"Dear God," he said out loud. "Dear God . . ."

When he came back later, Sargesson had packed his nose and changed his jacket for a windbreaker.

He didn't go into the cell, but moved around doing things in the annex. Now and then he stopped in the doorway to speak to Kemp, who was lying motionless on the bed with his eyes closed. He could have been asleep.

"You won't actually see me after today except through the grille. The setup here is pretty foolproof, really . . . both door locks are outside in the passageway and I only open one at a time. I never open either until I check on you first through a peephole. And having the extra utility room off here means you can look after yourself. But only while I'm here to keep an eye on you."

"Wait . . ." Kemp let his breath go. "Sarge, I don't know how this ever happened, but you have to check up on it further. You really must! Ask again around the place and you'll find the whole thing was a lie. Whatever reason she may have had, she was making the whole thing up. Ask her friends. . . ."

Sargesson had disappeared through the doorway again and drawers opened and closed. When he came back he said, "The walls are a meter thick, by the way. They were built for ammunition storage. I shall be watching you regularly, Kemp, and listening with my stethoscope to the outer wall."

Kemp with his eyes closed noticed that Sargesson was speaking more rapidly than usual and kept running out of breath. Sargesson seemed to be on some sort of high, and Kemp wondered for the first time whether he had succumbed to one of the temptations of the profession and taken something to turn himself on.

Sargesson said, "Maybe you're already thinking of how to find a way out, but you have to realize that it's quite impossible. There'll always be a locked steel door between you and the outside world. I gave considerable thought to the project, starting only two days after Marion died. It took me three months to find this place."

As the rambling voice paused for a moment, Kemp said sharply, "I had nothing to do with her death, Sargesson. You cannot convict me because Marion had a fix on me. You know what sort of obsessions adolescent girls can get and what they write in their diaries."

"Shut up, Kemp."

"If you really believe it then why don't you get the police and give them the evidence? . . ."

"That would dishonor her name."

"How long do you think you can get away with it?"

"Oh, for a lifetime . . . one of our lifetimes. A remission of sentence isn't really possible, is it?"

With a confidence he didn't really feel, Kemp said, "The police will find me in the end. The Bentley is a pretty conspicuous car . . . they'll start from there."

"I made you park outside the gates so there would be no tire marks in the driveway. There's nothing to connect the car with this house.

"Well, they'll start from wherever you dumped it."

Sargesson blinked and walked back into the service cell. After a long silence Kemp heard his voice more faintly. "It's really *very* important that you understand about trying to escape. Very important indeed. I must never detect you at it, because the consequences don't bear thinking about."

There was silence again. An oven door clanged. Kemp was straining at the bonds around his ankles to find a fraction of an inch of movement, but it was hopeless. He lay back.

When he opened his eyes, Sargesson was standing at the foot of the bed holding the scissors again. "And don't try to start a fire. There isn't enough inflammable material anyway, and even if there were, you would only suffocate. You did hear what I said about escaping, didn't you, Kemp? Unless you abandon all hope and resign yourself to a life of penance, I would have to . . . to take further means of restraining you."

"Okay, okay. You want to frighten me. So what would you do . . ."

"Well, it could only be some sort of chain which

would reduce you to the status of a dog, or else . . ."

"Or else what?"

"Well . . . surgery, I suppose."

Kemp didn't react for a moment, then he whispered, "You really are a crazy bastard, and that's the only thing that gives me hope."

"Bend forward, Kemp."

Keeping well away from Kemp, Sargesson leaned over to cut one of the canvas straps of the straitjacket with the scissors. "I just wanted you to know the penalties. And I'm not crazy, as you will slowly come to realize. The situation is completely rational. I can't bring you to public trial because it would dishonor Marion. I cannot kill you because of my Hippocratic oath. And your penance will be a penance for me as well. I shall have to devote my life to looking after you."

"You screwed-up sanctimonious shit!"

"I'm not screwed up, Kemp. As I keep telling you, it's all quite simple and rational. You've destroyed the meaning of my life and I intend to destroy the meaning of yours."

"Sarge, this whole thing is fucking crazy! You must listen to me. . . ."

Sargesson hesitated and then lowered the scissors, and after a moment Kemp half-straightened, watching him. Sargesson said, "I don't intend to go on discussing the matter endlessly. . . . I just want you to know the trial is over. But I'll quote you one piece of incontestable evidence, Kemp. On the thirty-first of October Marion wrote . . ." Sargesson hesitated, and then turned his head away. "She wrote, 'Jane's Hallowe'en party. Made it afterward with Peter Kemp. Fantastic!' "

The silence lasted a full half-minute before Kemp whispered, "Okay, so it happened once. I . . . I was sloshed. But I swear it was the only time. . . ."

Sargesson raised the scissors to a level with his blank face, and after another half-minute Kemp bent forward slowly again as if he were submitting his neck to the executioner's ax. Sargesson cut the second strap, but before Kemp could drag his stiffened arms clear of the sleeves the steel door of the cell had closed. He groped blindly toward it, like a puppet.

"I tell you that was the only time. . . . I never touched her again." He waited, listening, but there was no sound. "She went for me, Sarge. . . . I hate to tell you, but she was a tramp. She was hot for anyone with balls. . . . It was no secret. You must believe me!" He waited again, breathing heavily.

Then, from somewhere in the passage beyond, Sargesson operated whatever mechanism it was that sent the bolts trundling home.

Around three weeks later, when he was having lunch at the Auberge du Faisan Hardi, just up the road from the hospital, Josh came over to his table.

"You must have bought this place by now, Sarge."

"I prefer it to the hospital cafeteria." His bottles of *pastis* and wine both had his name scrawled across them with a felt-tipped pen. He pushed the *pastis* across to Josh. "Help yourself."

While Josh was still pouring, Claudine came with a carafe of ice water. Josh said, "What the hell's happened to Peter?"

Sargesson shrugged. "What do *you* think?"

"Well, I reckon the most likely thing is that he drowned. All his luggage was still in the car. Only the wet suit and his swimming gear were missing." Josh added more water to his *pastis*. "But why did he go to Brittany, after he'd told everyone he was going to Sicily?"

"A woman, maybe. They were his weakness, weren't they?" Sargesson helped himself to the cold vegetables and mayonnaise. He half-filled his glass with red wine. Then he added, "What are the police doing?"

"Oh, they've taken a few things from his room, and someone told Fran they'd sealed up his apartment. And they've taken statements from some of the junior staff." Then Josh said in a quieter voice, "You know, if you didn't cut yourself off from life so much, you'd know what was going on, Sarge."

"I wondered when you'd get to the point."

They waited while Claudine set the table with slices of Brie and Camembert and removed the vegetables. Then Josh said, "Well, I haven't really got there yet. ... What I really came to say was that Mary and I would like you to have supper next week. You can choose your company. We've got the American Consul from Marseilles on Wednesday, and Friday Geoff Mc-Cabe will be there."

"Sorry, Josh . . . can't make either."

A crowd of students came in from the American School farther around the Cap de Nice and sprawled at tables beyond them.

Josh said, "No good my giving you a little sound medical advice?"

"I don't think so."

"Well, I'm going to anyway. You can't just draw a line the way you're doing. Life has to go on, and in order for it to go on you have to feed it with some sort of social contact."

Claudine had left the bill with the cheese, and Sargesson put two ten-franc notes on his plate and added some small change.

"It's been six months now," Josh said.

Sargesson stood up abruptly. "Let's go."

He led the way out into the street, and a flock of pigeons rose jerkily and resettled again close to the pavement tables. They walked along under the pink and white façades back toward the side entrance of the hospital, and Josh said, "There's another thing, Sarge . . ."

"What's that?"

"Sometime we must talk about Mrs. Wallace Grant."

"Why not now? . . . Come up to my rooms."

When they arrived Josh worked his magic on someone nearby in the Pediatric ward, and shortly afterward one of the nurses appeared with two mugs of coffee. The mugs had rabbits on them, rabbits in nightdresses holding candlesticks. Josh sprawled on the examination couch with his, while Sargesson changed into his hospital jacket and made a phone check with Reception. There had been no calls for either of them.

"She's really your baby," Sarge said, still thinking of Mrs. Wallace Grant.

"Some baby!" Josh had his eyes closed and he went on to argue a proposition which was an endless cause of discussion between them.

Josh called it the *mens insana* syndrome and in general he postulated that physicians had outstripped the rest of the medical profession, bodies were living longer than minds, and in twenty years they would all be market gardeners and these twilit wards would be full of human vegetables. Mrs. Wallace Grant was the latest in a long line of examples and it was no good Sarge saying she was his, Josh's, baby. Her mind was worn out, and he had no cure for that. There was no spare-parts surgery in *that* field. He sat up and finished his coffee.

Sargesson said, "Mrs. Wallace Grant has contributed a quarter of a million dollars to the hospital rebuilding fund and it is the wish of the Governing Committee that she have the finest care." Josh put his cup down noisily on a corner of the desk, and for the first time Sargesson realized he was very angry.

"Fuck the Committee," said Josh.

As he opened the door, Sarge said patiently, "Please, Josh . . ." But Josh didn't look back.

In the silence after he'd gone, Sargesson continued to sip his own coffee, holding the mug at chin level. He hadn't really been listening to Josh; he had been thinking about Kemp's laundry, which was in the trunk of the car. He had sorted it out that morning. He decided he would take it to the laundromat in the shopping center at Cap Trois Mille, which was not far from the cemetery at Caucade. Pretty soon he hoped the laundry problem would be solved, when the parts the plumber was waiting for finally got here from the States. Meanwhile it wasn't too much of a chore, because while the washing was in the machine he could visit Marion's grave, which was something he liked to do regularly.

Right now it was time to check on Mrs. Wallace Grant. He put his stethoscope in his pocket and neatly stacked the two coffee mugs, taking them with him. One the way to the elevator he left them in the old-fashioned utility sink by the children's ward.

When he got up to Geriatrics, Fran was still away and another girl was standing in. She was a White Russian called Irina, from the agency in Nice, and she often did relief work in the summer. "Fran will be an hour," she said. "She is having her hair done. It is the only time they have free."

"Well, I don't want to see her specifically," Sargesson said.

"Have you heard?" Irina said. "They say there are units of the Sixth Fleet coming into harbor next week. They will be here five days."

"I shouldn't count on it, Irina. They don't usually advertise in advance."

"Will they come here? I mean Admissions . . ."

"I don't think so. They have their own medical facility with them. A while back they used to run the Path lab here and we even had a ward for Navy dependents, but not anymore."

"Oh." Irina was obviously disappointed. "Well, they'll be in town anyway," she said.

"I'll just take a look at Mrs. Wallace Grant while I'm up here."

"Do you want the history, Doctor?"

"No, I don't think so." And as Irina made to lead the way he said, "And I don't think I need bother you to come along."

"Oh." Irina had obviously sustained another disappointment.

He walked down the corridor of private suites to the one at the end, which faced west. Mrs. Wallace Grant was propped up in the bed, which was made up with her own embroidered linen. Her hair had been recently set and she wore a white angora jacket around her shoulders. He picked up the treatment chart, but there had been no new entries for a long time. The last was for two grams of Solastrium administered every four hours. It was written in Josh's scrawl and had been initialed by himself.

He put it back and moved around to sit on the edge of the bed. One of the flaccid hands moved immediately to hold his own, and Mrs. Wallace Grant spoke out loud, a dialogue that had already been going on in her mind. She was traveling with Simon on the train to Long Island, a trip with which he was familiar.

"Do you remember I would never again eat duck à l'orange, which had been one of my favorite dishes? Not after seeing those poor things. But *you* used to. I think the railroad company should insist that those . . . those farms should not be visible from the carriage windows. We all know the French do terrible things to geese, quite terrible, but one doesn't expect that in America. We are a rich country."

Her voice rambled on, answering its own questions, and after a while he was no longer Simon but someone else, God knows who, from her school days. When he made a slight movement, the dry claw that encircled his hand contracted sharply, and he thought of the Ancient Mariner.

He was also thinking about Kemp again and about his problems. He would have to have some better means of exercise than the pushups which he did three times a day, and Sargesson decided to buy a bicycle similar to the ones they had in the Therapy ward. He wouldn't let Kemp have it in his cell because Kemp's ingenious mind might devise equipment from it that would help him escape. It would only be available to him during his free period in the evening. That would be a start. Mrs. Wallace Grant stopped speaking as suddenly as she had begun and, looking at her, he saw that she had fallen into a light doze. He lifted her hand away and stood up.

When he was at the door she said loudly, "You'd better get the man to close the shutters now. It's very cold in here."

He went back to the ward office, removed her records from the file and made a note of his visit. Irina was reading an English novel, her lips moving with the words. Putting the file away, he said, "I want you to try to make her wear a hat or something on her head. That's where the heat loss is; she'll be much warmer. Tell Fran to buy some glamorous nightcap and charge it to her account."

"We really have tried, Doctor Sargesson. She says it spoils her hairdo."

"Well, tell her some story . . . say that it is a present from Simon and that he'll be very upset if she doesn't wear it."

"Well, we will try, Doctor. But Fran . . ."

"That's great."

"Is there any news of Doctor Kemp? Have they found anything yet?"

"I've no idea, Irina." He walked out quickly and headed for the main section. He wondered whether Irina had been one of Kemp's conquests.

He had the feeling that, along with the Sixth Fleet, he was a great disappointment to Irina.

There was only one person — a young girl — in the laundromat.

She was chewing bubble gum, and her jaws moved as rhythmically as the machine in front of her. After he'd programed his machine and started it up, he went out to the car and drove slowly back to the expressway, following the underpass through to Caucade. He walked briskly along the gravel paths, making for the lower end. Once, several months ago, he had seen the same family there that had picnicked on the day of Marion's funeral, but today there was no one but an elderly woman gathering sticks under a tree. While he was still quite a long way away, he picked out the small white slab that marked Marion's plot.

There was a metal vase by the headstone in which somebody, maybe Kemp, had left red roses a while back. He'd thrown them away, over the yew hedge nearby, and the vase had been empty since. He stood there with his foot on the marble ledge and, feeling the sun hot on his bared head, tried to think of her.

As he drove slowly up through the development that night, lights were coming on in the dusk, illuminating rooms with crisp log fires and tea carts laden with apéritif bottles.

The lights of cars driven by other commuters swept the gardens behind and in front of him. He reached the end of the cul-de-sac and switched off the engine. As he walked toward the solid iron gates he could hear the shrill voices of children quarreling in one of the houses nearby. Pushing back the gates, he smelled the familiar musty odor of rotting leaves and, looking up through the trees, he could just see the pilot light glowing in the portico. He drove the car in and switched off the engine and then locked the gates again. Out in the fields a dog was barking frenziedly.

He drove on through the tunnel of trees, circled the forecourt, and entered the open end of the storehouse and switched off the engine. In the abrupt silence he heard the rustle as a rat squeezed along under the tiles.

It was then he remembered the exercise bicycle. He had been going to look at one on the way home, at a sports shop in Beaulieu. He opened the car door slightly, put on the light, and wrote "exercise bicycle" in his diary in the space for the next day and returned the diary to the glove compartment. While he was writing, the rat, or another one, fell with a plop somewhere in the harness room behind.

Sargesson went around to open the trunk. He lifted out the laundry with care, closed the trunk with his elbow, and took the short cut through the trees to the house. In the offshore breeze the rattle of the long-stemmed aspen leaves was harsh and sustained and reminded Sargesson of night duty on a chest ward. The sound drowned his footsteps.

When he came out onto the forecourt, he suddenly saw that a man was standing under the light. For one heart-stopping moment he thought it was Kemp, that somehow he had gotten free, and then the Inspector moved forward.

"Doctor Sargesson? . . ."

"I'm sorry, I didn't see you there before."

"I was under the trees when the car arrived."

They both waited, still ten paces apart. At last Sargesson said, "It's kind of late, isn't it?"

"I'm sorry. I came at four-thirty. I telephoned the hospital, but you had left, so I came out here. Since you didn't arrive, I have been walking in the locality."

Sargesson started up the steps. "Is it really all that important? I'll be at the hospital tomorrow."

"Let me take that for you." Sargesson had been feeling for his keys and Peyrouse laid firm hands on the laundry. While he was opening the door the Inspector said, "I'd guess there are ten pounds here. You must have needed two machines."

"As a matter of fact, I used only one."

"You see, I also do my own laundry."

Sargesson took the bundle back again and put it down on the chest in the hall. "I thought you were going to Grenoble, to some course. Didn't you say . . . ?"

"That has been postponed. Something important has come along."

"Another case?"

"Yes. Another case."

Without removing his topcoat Sargesson walked into the front room, clicking on lights. He remained standing in the middle of the room. From the doorway Peyrouse said, "I came to tell you that the file about your daughter has now been removed from . . . from active consideration. It is nearly six months now, and I regret to say that only a little progress has been made."

Peyrouse took a notebook from his side pocket. It had a cover of tartan plastic. He didn't open it but kept tapping his open hand with the edge of it. "We found the motel, of course, where your daughter had been taken, but we were unable to identify the man. Only your daughter went to the office to pay the account and collect the key. It is necessary to pay in advance at such places. We assume the man to have been the abortionist."

Sargesson turned away. He started to undo the buttons of his coat. Behind him Peyrouse said, "You were aware that your daughter had a lover?"

Sargesson swallowed the ugliness before he said,

"After the manner of her death I naturally made that assumption."

"But you did not know *before* she died?"

"No." Sargesson peeled off his coat at last and carried it back to the hall. Returning, he said, "Can I offer you an apéritif?"

"No, *merci.*"

"Please . . ."

"Thank you, then I would like a *pastis,* if it is no trouble." And as Sargesson made to leave the room, he added, "Ice is of no importance. Let . . ."

"It's no trouble." Sargesson got it from the freezer, and when he came back Peyrouse was by the bookshelves. He was straightening from having replaced a book.

He said, *"Cherchez l'homme . . .* that is what we have tried to do without success. She was very discreet . . . your daughter."

He laid the notebook aside and took the glass from Sargesson, waiting until Sargesson had fetched his own. They drank, and then Peyrouse sat down on the edge of an overstuffed chair. "Only one thing we found out from one of her friends . . . she called him Peter. Do you know a Peter who was a friend of hers?"

"No." Sargesson hesitated and hoped his voice sounded natural. "No, I don't think I do."

"The possibility is that he is English or American . . . with a name like that." And Peyrouse repeated it. "Peter." He tasted his drink and set it down. *"Cherchez l'homme,"* he said again. "But we have not been successful."

Sargesson went away to add more water to his drink. "Well, thanks for letting me know. I greatly appreciate it."

When he returned, Peyrouse was sitting back in the chair opening the tartan notebook on his knee. "There was something else, Doctor Sargesson. . . ."

Sargesson waited, and Peyrouse, after glancing at the notebook, said, "Doctor Kemp was a friend of yours? I refer to the Doctor Kemp who is missing from the hospital."

"Well, I guess so. He's an associate."

"A *confrère* . . . ?"

"That's right. Do you have any news of him yet?"

Peyrouse hesitated. "No, nothing yet. His car was found near Finisterre, as you know. His clothes were in it but his mask and rubber suit were missing."

"Somebody told me. I thought . . . we all thought he was going to Sicily."

"He discussed his holiday with you?"

"I thought I heard him mention Syracuse. I don't know . . . some place down there."

"*Ah, oui.* Syracuse."

"If he was drowned the body would have come ashore somewhere surely."

Again the silence seemed to question him. Then Peyrouse said, "It need not always be so. The tides in the English Channel can run longer than usual under certain conditions, a strong wind in the same direction or a high barometric pressure. . . . It is a characteristic of the coast there that not all bodies come ashore with the current. In fact there is an old Breton saying, '*Les*

morts marchent par l'Atlantique,' — Dead men walk
the Atlantic. They are presumed to have been carried
away over the shelf, one supposes."

Sargesson waited through another silence but still
Peyrouse made no move to go. He went on talking in a
lowered voice almost as if he were talking to himself.
"There are two points which concern us. The first is
that he should have gone to the one place in France
where bodies are not always recovered from the sea. It
is almost as if he may be trying to deceive us. Perhaps it
is that he wanted to disappear, that he is not really
dead."

To avoid another silence Sargesson said, "Maybe, but
I shouldn't think it's likely. From his character and his
behavior here I would say it is much more likely that a
woman was responsible for his change of plan." He
hesitated. "You said there was something else. . . ."

"The car." Peyrouse glanced down at his notebook.
"One can tell by forensic method, as you know, who
has sat in a car and when, and so on. An examination
of fibers . . . My colleague in Brittany has found some
curiosities there."

Sargesson bent to pick up his glass. He said, "Well,
maybe that'll tell you whether he had a woman with
him."

"Perhaps," Peyrouse said vaguely. "Do you know
someone . . . a girl, called Miranda?"

Sargesson blinked. He turned away and put down his
glass. "No, I don't think so." And he added truthfully,
"I don't know any girl of that name."

"We have taken possession of several things from

Doctor Kemp's office and his apartment. In his office there was a desk pad for his daily appointments. Two entries last May and June have appointments that read ... that read ..." With tantalizing slowness Peyrouse let the pages of the notebook drift while he searched for the phrase. At last he said, *"Ah, oui.* Here's what he wrote on both those occasions. 'Give Sarge a lesson on Miranda.' You are sometimes called Sarge?"

"Oh that." Sargesson's short laugh was unconvincing. "I thought you meant some girl."

Peyrouse watched him steadily without smiling.

"Well, I can explain that okay. Miranda was what he called his old car. What happened was that I was considering buying one myself. They are technically very interesting, and they have a great club going for vintage cars over in Monaco. As a matter of fact Kemp was second in the *Concours d'Elégance* last year. So when I thought about it, I figured it might be a good idea to have a drive or two in his car first. It was just after my daughter died, and I guess I was looking for distraction. That's all it means."

"And did you find it easy to drive?"

"Well, not really. It was pretty heavy and finding the gears wasn't all that simple."

"But you managed to drive it."

"Yes, I managed. But I didn't buy one in the end. They come pretty expensive, as a matter of fact."

Peyrouse had started to write neatly in the notebook. To Sargesson's strained nerves he seemed to write for about ten minutes. Then, putting his pen away, he said, *"Ah, bon.* I must be exact, Docteur, because I am making a report for my colleague in Brittany. Naturally the investigation is being conducted there at the moment."

"Sure. I understand."

Peyrouse said, at last, "And now may I telephone from your house?"

"Certainly. It's on the landing. I'll show you."

He clicked on the landing light from the bottom of the stairs and Peyrouse ran lightly up. He opened the notebook again to read a number.

Sargesson went back into the living room, leaving the door open. Seeing his reflection suddenly in the pier glass, he was surprised by his untidy appearance. His hair was tossed this way and that, and he stroked it down. Beyond the door he heard Peyrouse speak one short sentence, a pause, then he said *"D'accord."*

The phone tinkled and a moment later Peyrouse called from the hallway, "The car is coming from the Gendarmerie. It is a fine night. I shall walk down to meet it."

Sargesson stepped out into the hall and lifted down a flash lamp from the shelf above the coatrack. "I'll see you as far as the gate . . . it's dark under the trees."

"Ah, bon." They went down the steps, and Peyrouse breathed deeply. "I particularly wanted to see the stars tonight. The configuration is interesting with Venus setting just after the sun. Are you interested in the stars, in navigation perhaps?"

"A little, maybe. I don't know all that much about it."

As they left the forecourt and walked into the whispering tunnel of trees, Sargesson heard the long wavering call of a barn owl somewhere on the hill above. It had something of the shrillness of a witch's warning. He pushed the button on the flash and the pool of light darted ahead of them.

"I only ask about the navigation, Doctor, because I noticed on your bookshelves the tide book of the *Service Hydrographique*. I thought you might practice sailing as a hobby."

Sargesson had to make a conscious effort to hold the flash steady. When he spoke, he knew his voice was unnaturally high, but there was nothing he could do about it. He heard himself saying, "Well, I used to have some sailing holidays with my daughter. . . . We did rent a small boat a couple of times. . . ."

"In Brittany?"

"Well, a bit farther north. Lately I thought I'd take it up again; that's why I got the tide book. It would be another interest."

"Like the old automobile."

Sargesson could not tell from Peyrouse's level voice whether he was interested or merely making conversation. He said, "Yes, like the Bentley."

They reached the iron gates and Sargesson opened them up. Going through them, Peyrouse said, "You need not trouble yourself further . . . the road has street-lamps to the bottom. Thank you for seeing me, Doctor. . . . I'm sorry that I came so late."

"That's okay." As a boxer senses a coming punch, Sargesson waited, knowing that there would be a final exchange. But although he was expecting it, the blow when it came still jolted him.

Peyrouse said, "He was not a . . . a particular friend, you said. He was, more exactly, a *confrère,* a *cher collègue.* I am speaking of Doctor Kemp."

"Well, something between the two, I guess. We saw each other at the hospital every day, but he was younger, of course."

"He called you 'Sarge,' I recall. In his notebook."

"That's right. Everybody calls me that."

Then Peyrouse said, "What did you call him?"

Sargesson's mouth opened and closed before the name would come out. "Peter," he said at last. Although he spoke the name quietly it was like a gunshot in the night, and like a gunshot in the night the silence after it seemed more complete than before.

Then Sargesson heard himself speaking with a wild rush. "Of course he was never a friend of Marion's, of my daughter. You should never think that. He wasn't *that* Peter. She knew him, of course, but he was a great deal older, you know."

"*Ah, bon,*" said Peyrouse, as if he didn't want Sargesson to go on. "And now my . . . *my confrère* is arriving." Two yellow headlamps were sweeping the houses as the car wound up the hill toward them. "Good night, Doctor."

Sargesson watched him walk down the middle of the road until he was suddenly caught in the glare. He started to wave a hand, the lights dimmed, and the car stopped.

Sargesson stepped back into the drive and locked the gates. He was more than an hour late.

Kemp would be wondering what had happened.

He had not slept well.

By four it was too late to take a sleeping pill, so he showered and dressed and went downstairs. After he'd made coffee, he went on down to the cellar to look at Kemp, but the cell was dark and silent. For a moment he wanted to wake Kemp up, give him a cup of coffee too, and talk. But Kemp would only have been abusive.

In the end he went back to the living room. He found the book of tide tables, which Peyrouse had put back on the shelf, and when he let the pages fall, it opened automatically at the Brittany section. He put it back and then took down one of the early Wodehouse novels and read until dawn.

He was early at the hospital; it was about eight, but there was already a message for him. It was from Inspector Peyrouse and asked if he could call at the Gendarmerie in Nice anytime during the day. After visiting the wards briefly, he drove around the point and down into the town.

The Gendarmerie was in an old building on the corner of avénue Maréchal Foch, near the St. Roch Hospital, where he sometimes went for consultations. Inside, the rooms were tall and dirty and smelled of years of officialdom. Sargesson waited at a desk while they sent for Peyrouse. A loudspeaker in a room nearby relayed a constant stream of radio talk. A patrolman down at the Gare Maritime was being asked to collect two kilos of fish for his sergeant's wife.

Then Peyrouse came. He shook hands briefly and led Sargesson away through a series of institutional corridors to his small, cramped office.

"Because I shall be going soon to Grenoble, they think this is all I need." He was tired and unshaven, and when he saw Sargesson looking at him he said, "Excuse me, Doctor . . . I haven't been to bed . . . another case." There was a signed wartime photograph of General de Gaulle on the wall behind him and a blow-up picture of a destroyer entering port. The window shutters were half open to the cool morning. "I had to ask you to come here because we have some property of yours, and there are tiresome regulations which say you must sign for it here in person."

Without curiosity Sargesson said, "What is it?"

Peyrouse leaned back in his chair and put his hands briefly over his face. "Do you think sometimes there are families, and people, who attract disaster? . . . The Borgias were like that and, in modern times, the Kennedys perhaps? And perhaps again, *you*, Doctor?"

"What do you mean? What's happened?"

"Your daughter died, your *confrère*, Doctor Kemp, is missing, possibly drowned. And now you have lost another friend."

"Who is it? What are you telling me?"

"I am telling you that a friend of yours is dead."

"Who? Someone from the hospital? Who are you talking about?"

"Her name was Liesel Schaffler."

"I'm afraid there's been some kind of foul-up, Inspector. I don't know any Liesel Schaffler."

Peyrouse opened the drawer of the desk and lifted out the gold sovereign locket case and laid it in front of him. "You recognize it, Doctor?"

"Yes. It was mine. I didn't know her real name."

There was silence in the room, the silence he had come to associate with Peyrouse. In the passage beyond a group of men tramped past rhythmically like a squad. "She died in her room out near the stadium at St. Maurice. I was called there last night. She left a letter for the authorities and in this letter she asked that this . . . this locket be returned to you, her good friend Sarge." Peyrouse lifted it by the chain. "Why did she kill herself, Doctor? Why did she do *that?*"

"I don't know. She told me once she wanted peace."

"And now she is eternally damned."

"I guess some people would say that."

Peyrouse averted his battered face. The stubble on his chin was streaked with white. "Her *carte* was in order, there was about ten thousand francs in her bank deposit book . . . and this." He picked up the locket by the chain again and sighed. "Is it very valuable?"

"I should think so. It's gold. It belonged to my mother."

The locket spun slowly at the end of its chain like a hypnotist's mirror. Sargesson watched it while he waited through another of Peyrouse's long silences. Then Peyrouse said, "Is it not strange that you should give an object of such value, both real and sentimental, to a prostitute whose name you do not even know? Isn't it an excessive fee for services rendered?"

And Sargesson, watching the locket still, felt the answer drawn from him as if he was in fact mesmerized. "But I did not give it to her for services rendered," he said slowly. "I gave it to her because I wanted to get rid of it. She just happened to be around at the time."

Walking back through the echoing corridors to sign the receipt book he said, "How did she die?"

"She was strangled."

"But I thought you said . . ."

"Oh, she did it herself with some electric wire. She tried to hang herself, but the police surgeon said the neck was not broken, the knot slipped, you see. . . ." And later, when Peyrouse had taken him back to the crowded entrance hall, he said, without expression, "Would you like to see her, Doctor?"

"I don't think so," Sargesson said. And he added, "Do you require me to?"

"No, it is not necessary."

After they'd shaken hands, he walked away up past the Notre Dame Church to where he'd parked his car by the station.

PART III

1

For six weeks there was no further sign of Peyrouse nor was there any word of the inquiry on Kemp.

The feeling of panic that had possessed Sargesson after his last interview with Peyrouse gradually subsided. It had been a needless panic, because Peyrouse's questions were really only random ones, which dealt with the circumstantial aspects of Kemp's disappearance. The tide book and the driving lessons had been explained quite plausibly, and he thought he was way ahead of Peyrouse on the question of forensics.

Then one morning a senior officer from the Gendarmerie in Nice called on the Committee Secretary to tell him that in the absence of any further evidence Kemp must be presumed dead from drowning. This was the conclusion of the police in Brittany, and the equivalent of a coroner's court sitting at Finisterre would shortly bring in such a verdict. The things taken from Kemp's office were returned in a carton, and arrangements were also being made to return the Bentley and its contents by flatcar from Finisterre. Kemp's family in New York, who were already in touch with the hospital, and the police had been advised. Later that day Tom Hurst, the retired British Naval Commander who was secretary of the Committee, had called a meeting of senior staff to inform them, and it was agreed not to advertise Kemp's position as Junior Physician in the *J.A.M.A.* but continue with local French doctors on a part-time basis. That night Sargesson had told Kemp all about it.

"So now, Kemp, you are officially dead. One of the chaplains, Barrymore as a matter of fact, is holding a short memorial service for you in the chapel on Thursday. I'll go."

It was the end of Kemp's evening period in the service room. There was a faint bitter smell of herbs and hot rice from some dish he had prepared. Sargesson had brought down the bucket and was about to take up Kemp's waste. They were facing each other's shadowy figures through the inspection mesh of the inner cell door.

Kemp said, "Don't you bloody well believe it." He went out of sight for a minute to put down the tray with tomorrow's food on it. After a moment he was back. "They never give up, Sargesson. They never, but *never*, close a file that hasn't been satisfactorily concluded. Someday someone else picks it up and gets a new angle. Or maybe someone turns in new evidence. . . ."

Sargesson could sense the desperation in Kemp's voice and knew that the news had really hurt him.

There had never been much hope, and Peyrouse snooping around had been the only thing going for him. Now it was over, and even Kemp couldn't keep it convincingly alive.

"They'll finally catch up with the abortionist and pull him in. He'll confess to Marion and half a dozen others in the file. . . ."

"They couldn't catch up with you, Kemp. Not here."

"Oh Christ . . . how can I ever convince you, Sarge, that you are totally wrong? . . ."

"Am I? Peyrouse has reached the same conclusion. He's looking for Peter too."

From the very first day that Peyrouse had called, Sargesson had discussed with Kemp every detail, real and supposed, of the police inquiry. They had speculated on the evidence of Kemp's death at Finisterre as if he had really been there and at other times they had considered the case against someone who had killed him and set him adrift in those racing tides that flooded through the Dover Straits from the North Sea to the Atlantic.

Just as it had helped to keep hope alive for Kemp, so in a different way did it help to ease Sargesson's anxiety. It was like confessing to a priest, because he spoke in the certain knowledge that whatever he said would never be communicated to another living soul. Kemp's cell had the inviolate sanctuary of the confessional, and the grille in the steel door and the shadowy figure beyond it helped to reinforce the illusion. And of course his present situation had one inestimable advantage over that of the confessional, an advantage that exhilarated him. Kemp could never give a penance. Whatever he said or did was unpunishable.

Meanwhile Kemp had returned to a favorite theme. "One way or another," he said, "the Bentley is the thing they'll get you on. You were never to know I'd make a note of giving you lessons on my reminder pad."

"But I've told you . . . I explained that to Peyrouse's satisfaction."

"Not really. You see there's something psychologically false about the evidence . . . something they can't quite figure. Maybe it's that you are not the kind of guy who would ever own a Bentley. It's out of character. And it's out of character for someone to approach the scene the way you did. You wouldn't go taking lessons from a junior. You'd have them instruct you wherever you bought the car. I don't know what it is, Sarge, but something there is bothering Peyrouse."

"Not anymore," said Sargesson quietly. "You forget . . . the case is closed."

"I don't think Peyrouse will give up." Again Kemp's voice was shallow with a lack of conviction. "The way he's been poking around proves that. He's really hooked."

"In a little while he won't be able to pursue the matter even if he wants to. They are sending him to Grenoble, as I told you."

"I wouldn't bet on it . . . decisions can get changed." Kemp had almost given up trying to convince himself. The shadow behind the grille vanished, and only bright digital squares remained where Kemp had stood.

He had taken the buckets to the kitchen and tidied everything up. Now he sat in the garish living room playing the music from *Singin' in the Rain.*

He sipped a glass of Armagnac, which was unusual, but then it was an unusual occasion. The investigation was over and he was untouched. Looking back now on Peyrouse's interrogation, he realized that all the suspicion and fear had really been in his own mind. Anyway, Peyrouse was finished now. Maybe he'd already gone to whatever course of instruction it was.

It was then, lulled by the music and mellowed by the Armagnac, and with the taste of triumph in his mouth that he decided to buy Kemp a sexual companion. In a paper somewhere, in some medical journal probably, he had read that such replica women were already a feature of advanced psychiatric therapy wards at some place on the West Coast. In downtown Nice there were several sex shops, and in one of them, which he often passed on his way to the British Library, he had seen discreet advertisements for just the same sort of thing. If Kemp couldn't exist without sex, then it was a more realistic way of achieving orgasm than masturbating.

Although he had thought of it as no more than that, the final outcome of what he considered to be a thoughtful gesture certainly surprised him.

Kemp's first reaction to Kiki had been predictable.

He had been angry and indignant. She was rejected the way everything else had been, like the exercise

bicycle, for example. After the first burst of indigna-
tion, Kemp had become scathing and facetious.

"I love you, my sweet inflatable you,
I love you, my sweet insatiable you,
Everytime you . . ."

Kemp had written a whole verse that disgusted Sargesson, which he sang loudly every evening during his
housekeeping period. But the facetiousness grew
weaker as the days passed by, and the weekend before,
when Sargesson had suggested he might as well take
her away, Kemp had come up close to the grille, where
Sargesson could see his face quite clearly.

Kemp said abruptly, "Kiki can stick around."

"As you wish, Kemp." Kemp's eyes, he noticed,
didn't quite come up to the level of his own.

Then Kemp added, "But you can take away her gear.
I don't have any hang-ups. Just leave her some
underclothes."

The next night during his free period Kemp had
hung a towel over the grille in the passageway door.
Sargesson was going to ask him to take it down but
stopped. He didn't want to be accused of voyeurism.

The really unpredictable thing happened about three
days later, again just as Sargesson was leaving with the
bucket. Through the grille Kemp said, "By the way,
Sarge, couldn't you buy Kiki some kind of dress . . . you
know, something to wear during the day."

"Well, maybe . . . I don't know."

"Oh, for Christ's sake. . . . How would you like to be
naked all the time?"

The next day had been market day in Beaulieu, so Sargesson had left the Basse Corniche and driven up there. At a covered stall he'd chosen a dress with stripes in two shades of a kind of bluey-lavender. It was a very respectable-looking dress, the sort he thought that Kemp had in mind. When he got home again that night he'd expected Kemp to be waiting eagerly.

But Kemp was asleep in a position that had become characteristic lately. His back was to the peephole and one hand rested on his shoulder. He flipped the hand irritably when Sargesson woke him.

"You're always asleep. You never used to sleep in the afternoons."

"It's Kiki. She's wearing me out. She's really a very good screw . . . better than some nurses I've had."

The dress was a little too big, but it was really smart, Kemp told him through the grille later. "I'll take up the hem tomorrow," he said. "Can you bring me a needle and some thread?"

"Okay, I'll try to remember."

"Make sure the thread's lavender."

Sargesson had been gone nearly half an hour, but Kemp stayed on by the grille. In the reflected light from his cell, he could just see Kiki, leaning against the wall of the service room where he'd left her. He stepped closer to the lattice so that he could see her face.

In a harsh whisper he said, "Good night . . . you beautiful chicken."

SARGESSON HAD PARKED HIS CAR, AND BECAUSE IT WAS A
bright morning he had walked the long way around to
the front entrance.

He was later than usual because he had no set appointments and the parking lot was already half-full.
He followed the line of oleanders and went up the steps
two at a time. Inside the vestibule he waved vaguely at
Mrs. Hackett, a British widow who was on Reception,
and headed for the elevator.

The next moment he was stopped dead. Mrs. Hackett
said, "There's someone called Kemp to see you,
Doctor."

His first thought was that it was Kemp who was
waiting for him. But even as he realized the impos-
sibility, Mrs. Hackett was saying, "*Mrs.* Kemp. I've put
her in your waiting room."

"Oh, thanks," he said and walked stiffly on.

As the elevator rose he thought about what he would
say to Kemp's mother. It did not fill him with particular

alarm, as he quite often had to deal with bereaved mothers in the course of duty. All the same, he didn't see why she had had to call on him. And then, walking down the long corridor with one hand spread and his case in the other, he realized of course that it could be no relation at all, but some patient with the same name referred to him. He opened the door to his consulting rooms and saw with relief that his supposition had been correct.

She was standing nervously by the window with her hands plunged into the pockets of a trench coat and she looked to be somewhere around the early thirties. She said quickly, "Doctor Sargesson? I'm Alicia Kemp. . . ."

"Do sit down, Mrs. Kemp. I'll be right with you."

As he walked on into his office, he saw her sit with a jolt on the edge of the nearest chair. He put his case down and hung up his light topcoat and jacket, then washed his hands and methodically broke open a fresh white coat. As he buttoned it up he opened the door and said, "Okay, Mrs. Kemp. . . ."

She came quickly into the doorway before he was around the corner of his desk. She said, "I'm sorry to bother you like this, but I'm Peter's wife. And I must talk to someone." She took a cigarette case with a flip top from her pocket, but immediately put it away again.

Sargesson said, with real surprise, "I never knew he was married. I don't think anybody here did."

"It was a long time ago," the girl said. "And it didn't take."

"I'm sorry."

"Oh, we had a sort of relationship." Mechanically she had taken the case from her pocket again and kept flicking the top with her thumbnail. "He always stayed with me when he came over to New York and once we met for a vacation in Scotland." There was a pause before she added, with irony, "I guess you could really say we were just good friends."

She had put the cigarette case away again, and again she kept her hands plunged deep in her trench coat pockets. Close to, she had a narrow sensual face with dark, thick lashes. And under the trench coat her body was angular, angles which constantly changed as she moved from one stance to another. Automatically, as if she were a patient, he had opened his desk diary. Now he closed it again, as he considered courses of action.

He heard her say wildly, "I had to talk to someone, you see . . . someone who knew him . . . who understands."

Like an echo from his conversation with Peyrouse, Sargesson heard himself say, "Well, we weren't all that close. He was an associate, of course, but . . ."

"He mentioned you a couple of times in his letters. And so when they told me the secretary wouldn't be in today I thought . . ."

Sargesson stood up again and took off his hospital coat. As he hung it up carefully and took down the jacket of his suit, he said, "Well I'm certainly glad to give you any advice I can. But I think we might be more comfortable at the café along the street. *You'll* be able to smoke and *I* shan't be disturbed."

"Oh that's wonderful of you, Doctor . . . I can't tell you how truly grateful I am. Since I arrived a couple of nights ago I've been in such a state . . ."

He moved around the blind side of the desk to the window and said, "Can you come here a moment . . ."

As she leaned toward him, looking out, he smelled her scent, which was sharp and somehow masculine. "It's the Faisan Hardi, almost on the corner. There's a sign with a pheasant on it, but it's kind of faded now. There are tables outside. There are also tables in the garden, where we'll be less disturbed. Would you mind waiting for me there? I have to see the head nurse and someone else first, but I shan't be long."

He showed her to the door and went back to the window again and waited. After two or three minutes she appeared from the direction of the main entrance, and he saw her stop immediately to light a cigarette. She walked on quickly, throwing her head back as she inhaled the smoke.

Sargesson pressed the intercom on his desk and spoke briefly to Fran Olsen. He'd be in later, unless she had any problems right now.

She said, "No problems, Sarge," and she added sweetly, "We're getting pretty good at running things ourselves." He knew she was critical of the time off he'd been taking lately, but he didn't want to discuss it then and there. He closed the switch, flipped another, and told Mrs. Hackett he was going out.

"Can I reach you anywhere, Doctor Sargesson?"

For a moment he hesitated, then, "No," he said, "I'm afraid that won't be possible." He hesitated again before leaving the room and then took his topcoat. Going down the driveway, he laid it over his arm.

She was sitting at one of the bench tables with her

face up toward the sun. Beneath the clear lipstick he could see the coarse indentations of her lips, as remote as the surface of the moon. She said, "It's so warm here. I don't wonder Pete was crazy about it."

"It's not always like this."

Claudine had followed him out and they shook hands. When he introduced her to Alicia Kemp, he saw Claudine's eyes sharpen with interest.

"What would you like?" he said.

"What are you having?"

"Oh . . . coffee, I think."

"Could I have a brandy? I need something stronger than coffee."

"Surely."

Claudine had understood and was already going back to the bar. Sargesson noticed that Mrs. Kemp had finished her first cigarette and had lit another. He said, "If you're finding the present situation is causing you too much stress, I'm sure we could prescribe something. . . ."

"Thank you, but I've got . . . I've got what I need."

He sat down with his back toward the street and put his hands in front of him on the table as if declaring that he was unarmed. She said, "There's just so many things to deal with . . . you know, papers, and that stupid British car. . . ."

A boy had brought the drinks carefully along the gravel path on a tray. Alicia Kemp turned her chair sideways to the table and crossed her legs. One slim knee was aimed at him through the flap of the trench coat. The brandy was in a tulip glass, and the hungry mouth had swallowed half of it before the boy was back in the bar.

He said, "What still surprises me is that Kemp . . . Peter . . . never told us he was married."

Mrs. Kemp said, "And you're also surprised that I'm quite a bit older than Pete."

"Well . . ."

"It was the little boy that got me. Maybe he had a touch of the Oedipus as well."

Sargesson said carefully, "He hasn't . . . displayed the same choice around here. He's played the field."

She finished her brandy and smiled at him through her thick lashes. "It was all over before it began. I found out in the first month that he was a traveling man." Absently she flipped the rim of the empty glass with a nail the way she had flipped her cigarette case.

"Why did he marry you? If he was just a womanizer . . ." Sargesson surprised himself at the ease with which he spoke of Kemp in the past tense.

"Well, that's something that bothered me, too, in the beginning. And in the end I think the answer was that it was me married him. I was lonely then. The way I am . . ." Her voice died abruptly. She said, "I'm talking too much. Do you think I could have another brandy?"

"I guess so."

He turned and held up a hand, and someone must have been watching from the darkness of the bar because the boy appeared almost immediately. As he came down the path she said, "Why don't you have one . . ."

"No, thank you."

"Oh come on . . . freshen up that coffee." And before Sargesson could say anything else she had signaled the boy with two fingers. "Two brandies."

Sargesson didn't look up. He heard the boy call softly, *"Oui, Madame."* Then he said slowly, "Well, I guess strictly speaking I'm not on duty."

This time when the boy had brought them, Sargesson asked for a dish of stuffed olives. While they were coming, he said, "The oil helps to regulate the absorption of the alcohol. That's what I always say, but maybe it's just I like olives."

"That figures," said Alicia Kemp, and laughed softly.

A bread van arrived at the front of the restaurant and a man in blue working clothes carried armfuls of long French loaves through the garden and around to the kitchen at the back. Sargesson had been waiting for an opportunity to depersonalize the conversation, to escape to some neutral ground. He started to tell her about the Faisan Hardi, how they shared the business, how Claudine's husband did the cooking.

"I like that," Alicia Kemp said. "I think that's a great arrangement."

"Unfortunately the sharing doesn't go any farther." Even as he said it he realized it was a mistake. They were back in the field of personal relationships again. He swallowed a mouthful of laced coffee. It was bland and bitter, the way cough mixture had been when he was a child.

"Well that's life." Then she added, "Share today, gone tomorrow," and laughed again. She had a pleasant throaty laugh, and Sargesson smiled in spite of himself.

She said, "Do you know that was really the first time I've laughed in three long days? I haven't laughed since the day I got here."

"You've been here three days?"

"Well, two days. . . . I got here the day before yesterday. I was wiped out the first day with jet lag. I had a key to Pete's place, and I just went up there and passed out. And yesterday the whole thing just got to me. . . . I just couldn't call anybody. I went down to the parking lot and looked at that antique monster. . . . What am I going to do with it, for Chrissakes?"

Sargesson said, "We have a firm of notaries who deal with our affairs at the hospital. I could arrange for them to see you if it would be any help."

"Oh, don't talk to me about the legal part! This lawyer in New York told me to just tidy up all his stuff, papers and so on, and keep the receipts for anything I sell . . . like the goddam car. What happens is that it is all tied up so that it goes to his mother, then when she dies it comes to me. I really don't understand it, so let's not talk about it."

For some time, ever since they'd got the last drink, in fact, he had been aware of her crossed leg kicking occasionally, almost as if he had been testing her reflexes with random taps. There was some quality of irritated impatience about it, as there had been when she played with her cigarette case.

She said, "How do you sell a thing like *that* . . . I mean the car." The knee jerked restlessly.

"I believe there's a dealer in Monaco who trades in vintage cars. I can find out his name and let you know. . . ."

"Oh, could you? That would be wonderful." She finished her glass and put it down, turning the base slowly around. She looked up at him through her lashes in the way she had and said, "I guess we'd better not have any more."

He smiled and shrugged, and was aware again of her jerking leg. She said, "It would be terrible to get plastered. Things happen when I get plastered."

Sargesson said, "And I can't, anyway. This place is pretty close to base."

"We could move on."

The silence while she waited, watching him, seemed as shrill with warning as the cry of the owl on the hill the night Peyrouse had been questioning him. The brief moment of arousal that he had felt was not only due to her hungry mouth and the leg flexing and unflexing beside him, but it had also, obscurely, something to do with Kemp.

He heard himself say, "Well, I do know a place downtown where they're not likely to track me down." He lifted a hand for the boy and while he waited he added, "They have pretty good food there, too."

She didn't say anything but just smiled at him brightly. Then for the first time he realized with a shock that she'd already had a little more than the two brandies he'd bought her. After he'd paid the bill he said, "I'll get the car and pick you up outside."

Again she smiled and nodded.

Crossing the square with his wrists bent and his hands spread, he rejected the whole idea. When he got back to the hospital, he'd call up Claudine and ask her to give Alicia Kemp a message. He'd say that he'd had an emergency call and he couldn't make it back and would she call him tomorrow. He'd go to Reception and phone through right away. Maybe it would be better if he got Claudine to bring Kemp's wife to the phone and he'd explain it himself.

But all the time he was telling himself this he'd turned away from Reception and was crossing the parking lot to the Peugeot. He climbed in, fitted the key into the ignition switch, and again hesitated. In the end he climbed out. He walked back through the lines of cars and out the side entrance again. Under the plane trees opposite, two cabs waited. He got into the first one.

As they drew up at the Faisan Hardi he opened the door and said, "I thought a cab was best because they don't have anything like enough parking space downtown. It is a real problem all along the coast here."

She climbed in beside him and looked at him with the same silent smile. They went to a place where he had once gone with Fran Olsen, a set of rambling cellar rooms. The walls were banked with old wine vats and the bar was built into what had once been an enormous press. The carpets subdued the noise and dim lights subdued vision. It was an atmosphere that softened all emotion.

They sat in deep dark chairs made from barrel staves. Alicia Kemp had taken off her trench coat at last, and beneath it she wore a loose blue dress, which again seemed only to touch her bones. The waiter, in keeping with the decor, was fatherly and reassuring. Alicia decided to stay with brandy while Sargesson ordered a *pastis.* They had the usual humorous exchange when he specified without ice water, and the waiter lit her cigarette with the deference of a court chamberlain before going off to the bar.

When they were alone she said, "I like this place." And she added, "Nice is nice," and gave one of her low-register laughs.

In the darkness Sargesson didn't need to smile. He wanted to talk but could think of nothing to say. He'd never been good at bedside small talk. In the end he said, "Do you have a job back there? Did you have any problem getting away?"

"No problem. I work at the Lenox Hill Hospital . . . on the children's ward. And I have an apartment around the corner on East Eighty-sixth, which I share with another girl. It's big enough so we don't get in each other's way." She swallowed half her drink. "And I have a boyfriend who's a librarian downtown who has no intention of marrying me. I suppose you could say I'm just the average American big-city girl." Again she laughed. "Hey! What do I call you, anyway?"

"I'm called Sarge by most people."

"Hey, I like that. I've never known anybody called that before. And I remember now that's what Pete called you in his letters." She had taken another cigarette from the case and before she had it to her lips the benign figure was there, bent over her as if he were offering the sacrament.

"Why, thanks . . . *merci.*" And as the waiter went she said slowly, "And do you live right here . . . at the hospital?"

He also could have said, he thought dryly, that he shared a place with another man and that *they* didn't get in each other's way. "No, I have a place along the coast. There's a room at the hospital which I can use when I need it. I don't have a wife, and I lost my only daughter a while back." The dimness seemed to soften the memory as it softened everything else.

"Pete told me about it in a letter. I recall he was very upset . . . he felt he was partly to blame." She tapped her cigarette in the ashtray, rocked her glass to and fro, unaware of the stillness she had created.

Sargesson said, "Maybe he was."

She said casually, "Well, he was pretty busy at the time. . . ." Her voice died away, and he was aware of her crossed leg jerking in its nonvolitional way again. Her mind was somewhere else.

There had been only a scattering of people in the darkened rooms, but now tables around them started to fill up and waiters were passing softly with trays, and when he asked for a menu the elderly waiter took their order.

She looked across at him. "Are you okay, Sarge?"

"Okay," he said. And he added, "Enjoying myself, in fact. I haven't had a day off like this in quite a time."

"It's not over yet."

After they had eaten lightly of onion soup and chicken Marengo, they had more brandy with their coffee. Alicia was ecstatic about the meal. "I've never had chicken like that before . . . it was fantastic! Once in New York I had it with Pete, but it was completely different."

"There are different versions of the way Napoleon's chef did it. Here they do it with Chambertin, which seems to be the only wine he carried around with him on his campaigns."

She wasn't listening again, he could tell, and suddenly she had leaned low across the table toward him. In the half light her thin face looked like a sculpture. She said tensely, "Will you come back to the apartment with me? Please say you will . . . it really got me down there yesterday. If you come back with me once, maybe it would be okay . . . that would lay the ghost." The words came rushing out of her, and he knew she had been thinking about saying it for a long time.

While he hesitated, looking into the tilted dregs of his coffee, she said quickly, "You've been very kind to me already and I won't bother you again after this. I promise it."

Because he was pretty sure of what he was going to commit himself to, he still hesitated. But there was something exhilarating about his hesitation all the same.

"Please," she said. When he looked up at her she was shaking her hair away and dashing her wrist across her eyes. In a weary voice she said, "Oh, shit . . ."

He didn't know whether her distress was genuine or not, but he said mildly, "It's okay. I'll come back with you."

She left her seat and hurried off through the tables. It was as if he had released a spring; the sharp bones of her body moved like clockwork beneath the loose dress. He stood up and went the opposite way to the men's room. In the distant bar that it opened out of, a color TV was blazing from an open barrel. Two men in white were showing a man with a microphone through endless corridors of machinery. It was the eternal theme of French television — a mindless compulsion to inform people about the wonders of technology. He went on in to have a pee in a pan where the flush didn't work.

Then he splashed cold water on his face and stayed for a long moment watching his dripping reflection before he pressed it dry with a paper towel. He'd got off, there was no doubt about *that*. It was a long time since he'd coupled with a woman. The last time had been at a conference in New York, where it was one of the amenities. But he wasn't sure what was exciting him. Was it the thought of ravishing Kemp's wife? That he would be getting back at Kemp? He would be able to tell Kemp about it, of course, and for a moment he could imagine himself again at that confessional grille whispering the details to Kemp's shocked face. When he went out again, the man with the microphone was in close-up, telling everyone what a wonderful experience it had been. The technocrats stood smugly in the background, one of them cleaning his bifocals slowly, like a cat cleaning its whiskers. Back at the table, she hadn't sat down but was waiting, with her hips slanted and that curious smile on her face.

A cab lurched forward as they came out into the bright glare of the afternoon, and Sargesson gave the driver the address of Kemp's apartment. He had been there several times before, to small parties, and twice of course when he had gone around to have a lesson on driving the Bentley. Alicia had the keys out of her bag before they'd reached the elevator, and they rose slowly to the third floor, still without speaking. She opened the apartment door and dropped the keys into a china bowl on the chest in the hall. There was a carton just inside the door, full of papers and taped across with a lot of blue tape. Sargesson, bending briefly to look at it, saw that the label was rubber-stamped with the office of the Gendarmerie in Nice. They had also returned the things taken from his apartment when the investigation ended.

Alicia Kemp had stripped off her trench coat and gone into the living room. When he reached the door she was lifting the lid of the silver cigarette box, but almost immediately she closed it again and went to the cabinet where the drinks were. There was a disarray of bottles standing on it.

She said, "What'll it be?"

"The same, I guess . . . cognac and water. Don't make it too big, though." She poured two drinks carelessly into tall glasses and came back toward him. She put them down on the mantelpiece behind him, among some of Kemp's sporting trophies. Then she turned, laying her hands on his shoulders.

"Hi, Sarge."

"Hi."

They kissed gently several times and after about half a minute he felt the hungry mouth open under his. Her hands fell slowly down his body. She stepped away at last and said, "I don't really need that drink."

She crossed the room and opened the bedroom door

and went in without closing it, and a moment later her dress sailed through the air and fell in a heap at the foot of the bed. Then the room dimmed as she drew the curtains.

Sargesson undressed hurriedly where he stood, putting his clothes methodically across a wing chair. As he reached the door of the bedroom in his shirt, she said, "If your patients could see you now . . ." She was stretched out on the bed, the sheet just touching her breasts and bones the way her clothes had done. She twitched the sheet away as he reached the side of the bed. He knelt beside her and after a moment stood up again and went through the door nearby into the bathroom.

She twitched the sheet back again and waited with a knee swinging restively. A faucet ran, stopped, and started again. She called, "Sarge?" but he couldn't have heard her.

After another couple of minutes she muttered, "Oh for Christ's sake," and rolled out of the bed again. As she went toward the bathroom she said, "*You* don't need anything . . . it's all taken care of. . . ."

Then she saw him, and her dry scream went on and on. It was as ear-splitting as a long blast from a siren. Until at last she stopped it with her knuckles.

The blood-splashed face just went on staring back at her. After a while she heard his choked voice through the sponge. "It's all right," he was saying. "It's really quite okay. Just a nosebleed. . . . I get them occasionally." She slammed the bathroom door before he'd finished speaking.

It was a worse one than usual and even pinching his nose through the cold sponge didn't help and he could feel the blood pouring down the back of his throat as hot and thick as soup. He groped his way through the bathroom cabinet but couldn't find any cotton, and in the end he had to pack it with toilet paper. It was around fifteen minutes before he carefully changed the packing for a smaller one and started to clean himself up with the sponge. Then he wiped out the basin.

He moved slowly, feeling beaten and embarrassed. What in hell had gotten into him? Why did he ever agree to let that slut bring him back here? From the mirror above the basin the Puritan face stared back at him in disgust.

In the end he opened the door and went through. With relief he saw she wasn't in the bed, and he went on to the living room. He could see her head over the back of a chair and a cigarette in the ashtray beside it. He said weakly, "Sorry . . . guess I've loused it up."

She stood to face him. She was wearing the trench coat again and there were two bags by the door. "I can't stay in this dump. Will you call me a cab? I can't make the fucking phone work, either."

The wall phone was by the door. There was a tray The line was dead. He said, "It's disconnected. . . . The concierge will have one, though. Would you like me to . . ." But she already had a suitcase in either hand and was making for the outer door. "Where will you go?"

"A hotel. . . ." She put down one bag and picked up the key from the china bowl and put it in her pocket.

Then she went out, closing the door with her foot.

He stood there looking at the door and then down at the carton which the police had left. Then he went over to the long window. After a moment he saw her walking down the middle of the road until she was overtaken by a Mercedes cab.

He went back to the bathroom. This time when he changed the packing there was only a little blood-stained mucus. He made an even smaller packing, then went back to put on his clothes. With his topcoat buttoned up, the bloodstains on his shirt weren't visible.

Then he took his topcoat off again and laid it over the back of a chair. He started to tidy the apartment methodically, emptying the glasses and rinsing them, stacking the bottles in the cabinet, putting the covers back on the bed. Then he picked up the carton by the door and put it on the table. He gently tore off the official tape which crossed the open top of it and lifted out the various things the police had taken away for examination.

The pad for the telephone was there and for whatever reason two pairs of Kemp's shoes. Then there were several Government Service envelopes. He picked one up that was labeled, "Contents of Letter Box." He opened it. Inside, the envelopes and letters were neatly clipped together. Sargesson flipped over an electricity bill and found a couple of letters. One was from a New York bookshop regretting they couldn't supply whatever book it was that Kemp had ordered, and the other was from Josh Weiss. Sargesson recognized the writing immediately. It had been folded and refolded, he noticed, and when he opened it out he could see the outline of the clips that had held it in the photocopier. The police had thought it important enough to copy, then. He sat down on the edge of one of the wing chairs before he read it.

Dear Pete,
(Josh had written in his fly-away handwriting)
No it wasn't unethical of you to discuss Sarge with me. Get that right out of your head. Since Marion's death, which must have been a severe betrayal to him, I've been pretty worried myself, for reasons I can't go into here.

If he's interested in the Bentley, great — push it! Anything that externalizes his interest is a help. And I shouldn't worry too much about the work side either. The reason he's letting up there is that the new house is keeping him busy, which is also a good thing.

Hope you have a great fortnight — don't fail to visit the Villa Communale at Reggio if there's time before your ferry sails.

See you (maybe at Barney's tonight),

JOSH

Sargesson read it twice. He knew that Peyrouse must also have read it before coming to question him. Peyrouse had known that his friends were worried about him. And what had Peyrouse made of the word *betrayal*? And, for that matter, what the hell did Josh mean, anyway? He wondered whether Peyrouse had interviewed Josh about the letter. Whatever conclusion they might have reached was irrelevant now. The investigations were over.

He put the letter back again behind the letter from the New York bookshop and put everything back in the envelope and dropped the envelope into the carton. He didn't bother with the tapes. As he let himself out of the apartment some old clock was dinning out the hour. It was four.

He collected his car from the lot behind the hospital without seeing anyone. Before he reached the lower Corniche, he pulled to the curb and got out his notebook. It was the day he shopped at the supermarket at Cap d'Ail, and he briefly checked the list. Then he drove on. He drove fast, spurred by his anger and remorse. That he should have been such a stupid bastard! What had gotten into him! He didn't even like the woman. And to begin with, he knew that what had driven him on had been the idea of hurting Kemp.

Then at the moment of entering the bed, something had happened. He had realized with a kind of nausea that it was the woman he wanted to hurt. He drove on with his mind a mélange of confused emotions.

BACK AT THE HOUSE HE'D SORTED OUT THE SUPERMARKET bags on the kitchen table, putting his own things away in the pantry.

Then he went upstairs and changed his shirt before going down and mixing his cocktail. He made a White Lady with care, and from the records on the stand he chose an old Ray Noble selection which started with "Tiptoe through the Tulips." Then he moved around the room with his hands hung out to dry as usual, and slowly, for the first time since leaving the apartment, he started to relax.

He'd never kidded himself about his regression. He knew that this trip back into the past, which he took more and more often since Marion died, nightly in fact, was a return to the only great time he had ever really known. It was just before the war and he was fifteen . . . sixteen, and everybody loved each other. His mother mixed the cocktails then and he was allowed a very small one, and she'd also played the music on an old

Victrola. He could hear it now behind the Ray Noble orchestra, just as he could smell the Abdullah ciga-rettes and feel the warmth of total security. Some part of him had always stuck there, in the years before the war, and it was where he always went back to. Always. After his mother died, postwar, after the fuck-up of his marriage, after Marion's death. One day when he re-tired, he'd stick there altogether and just skip the rest of the world.

He freshened his drink and carried it out to the kitchen, leaving the music playing. Then he got Kemp's clean buckets from the back room, filled the lavatory one with water and a shot of formaldehyde. Kemp was always complaining about the smell of the formalde-hyde. He failed to understand that a man with modern plumbing does not continually buy commercial sol-vents for a chemical toilet. It would not be natural, and, if noticed, would be a matter for curiosity. He went down to the cellar. When he withdrew the plug and slipped the periscope through the hole he saw Kemp doing pushups beside the bed.

There was sweat on Kemp's naked back, which had been bronzed by the sunlamp. Not for the first time he thought that Kemp bore more than a passing re-semblance to Jeremy Stuart, who had moved into his old apartment. Sargesson watched him for several min-utes until he'd reached the end of the sequence and relaxed, his body heaving on the cement floor. He really couldn't figure how Kemp, who was quite a handsome guy, became involved with that coarse bitch he had met today. He withdrew the mirror at last and started spinning the wheel that opened the door into the service room. Kiki was in the usual place, where Kemp had started to leave her lately, sitting astride the exercise bicycle in a realistic way, and before Sargesson had put down the buckets, Kemp was at the grille.

Sargesson saw his fingertips come through and flatten as he grabbed it. "Sarge?"

"Hi."

"Have you got it? Have you got the thread?"

"The thread . . ." Sargesson couldn't remember.

"The thread for her dress. Christ . . . that's all you had to remember."

"I'm sorry . . . it was a tough day. I forgot. . . ."

But Kemp's fingertips had gone and Sargesson could hear him shouting abusively as he moved around the cell. He went upstairs again for the food, and when he came down Kemp was back at the grille. "Promise me you'll get it tomorrow, Sarge. I really need it. I was going to do it tonight. I'd planned it that way. Maybe there's some upstairs?"

"No."

Kemp sighed. "Okay then. Tomorrow."

Sargesson left the paper bag with Kemp's groceries on top of the refrigerator and went back to the grille. "I . . . I met someone you know today."

"Who was that?"

"Alicia."

There was silence for a moment, then Kemp said, "You've got it wrong. I don't know any Alicia."

"She said she was your wife."

"Oh Christ . . . *Alice!* Is that what she's calling herself." Kemp laughed. "Why is she here? Is she looking for me?"

"She's come to collect your personal belongings and ship them back to the States."

Kemp was silent again.

Sargesson said, "You never told us you were married, Kemp."

"I didn't regard it as anyone's business but my own. Does she think I'm dead?"

"Everyone thinks that." Then in a lighter voice Sargesson added, "She's finding the Bentley quite a problem."

"Poor Miranda. I suppose some bloody dealer will buy her." Again Kemp sighed. "Anyway, what did Alice want with you? . . ."

"Oh, the Commander was away, so she came to see me instead. I . . . I gave her some advice. I'm going now, Kemp. I've got a can of cassoulet in the oven." He went out, closed the outer door, and then released the bolts of Kemp's cell door.

Upstairs, the record had finished, and he turned it over before pouring another drink. Then he took his notebook from his pocket and wrote "lavender thread" at the bottom of the notes for the following day.

The music hadn't started and the needle was still hissing when Sargesson heard, far off in the landscape beyond the window, the deep baying of the farm dog, followed by the death rattle of its chain.

"You've cut your hair." Sargesson was aware of reproach in his voice. He'd rather liked Kemp's hair when it was longer and curling at the neck like a drake's tail.

Kemp had already cut it two or three times before, using the scissors and a sort of comb-razor combined, which Sargesson had bought at a drugstore. He checked now that both items were back on the hooks where they belonged, and when he picked up the slop bucket he saw swaths of Kemp's thick hair floating on the top.

From the grille, Kemp said seriously, "I think Kiki prefers me looking butch."

"Oh, for Christ's sake . . ." Sargesson was following his usual routine of counting off everything against a checklist on the wall.

As he went out at last, carrying the bucket, Kemp said loudly, "Don't forget the thread tomorrow. Lavender."

Kemp heard Sargesson close the door and spin home the bolts. For half an hour he jogged, to and fro, the length of the cell. Finally he stopped at the grille again. For a long time he stared through at Kiki sitting astride the exercise bicycle in the dim reflected light.

"Okay, Baby?" His voice was solicitous. "How's the jack? Not too uncomfortable tonight?"

ON THURSDAYS HE ALWAYS DEALT WITH CASES REFERRED
to him from within the hospital.

It was the day most convenient for consultations,
because hardly anyone took Thursday off, and the
French doctors from the neighborhood who had patients there usually made it then. It meant a long morning in the wards, and after lunch he saw in his office
those who weren't bed patients. There were only three
that afternoon, two pregnancies and a postoperative
case. He was seeing the last woman out when he was
aware of another patient, a man, immersed in a newspaper. As he closed the door and turned back, Peyrouse
folded the paper and put it on the seat beside him.

"Doctor . . ."

Sargesson could feel his heart beating a little faster.
He waited for a moment before he said, with a half-
smile, "*Another* case, Inspector?"

"*Ah, non. . . .*"

"I thought the other one was dead."

And like the echo of Kemp's voice in the cell he heard Peyrouse say somberly, "Only the victims die . . . investigations never die."

"Unless they're solved."

"Unless they are solved."

Sargesson led the way into the examination room and while he settled in his chair Peyrouse laid a fat dossier on the desk and then began walking idly around the room. His eyes moved along the reference books and catalogues on a shelf and dropped to the glass case of equipment underneath. Then he turned back to face Sargesson. Sargesson waiting had the same apprehension as always, that of facing a fencing opponent and not knowing from where the lunge would come. Only that it would come suddenly.

But even though he was expecting it, he was still shocked when Peyrouse said, "Tell me, Doctor . . . was Doctor Kemp a sexual deviant?"

Sargesson's first confused thought was of Kiki, a police agent in the shop, maybe, but of course *that* was crazy. *Nobody* knew. He stared down at his pad where the indentation of his last prescription was still visible, and he must have been silent so long that Peyrouse said, "Perhaps my English word is incorrect. I have not consulted Larousse."

"No," Sargesson said. "I know what you mean." He hesitated. "It's just that it's such a crazy question. He always seemed pretty normal to me."

Peyrouse laid his small hand on the dossier. "It is only that it would have offered the possibility of a solution to his death." Peyrouse waited, using the silence as he had done on previous occasions, as other interrogators used words.

At length Sargesson said, "I'm afraid I don't get it."

Peyrouse took his hand from the dossier and joined it to his other hand in an attitude of piety. "I told you when we met before, Doctor, that there were certain curiosities about the report from the forensic laboratory."

"You mentioned them but you didn't say what they were."

Peyrouse looked down at the temple of his hands, his expression concentrated as if he was trying to remember the precise words of some catechism. "It was the car, you remember. The condition of the interior revealed that no one else had driven it, only Kemp."

"Well, that's what you'd expect, isn't it?"

Peyrouse waited again without looking up. A full half-minute went by before he said, "Only the fibers of Kemp's clothing and only his fingerprints and the prints of his gloves were found. That is what you would expect. What was unexpected was that the microscope revealed that the saline content of the body particles in his clothing was higher than usual." Peyrouse had lifted a page of the typescript. "Also there was an unusual compression of the fibers where the joints touched the fabric and in his socks. And then they found traces of white powder. . . ."

Sargesson said dryly, "I can assure you Kemp didn't use face powder. If that's the reason . . ."

"*Ah, non.* It wasn't face powder; it was the powder that some divers use to ease the fitting of a rubber suit and the findings permitted only one answer. Doctor Kemp drove his car across France wearing a rubber suit under his clothes. That is a curiosity. And it is often a sexual abnormality for people to wear rubber suits when they are not swimming. That is the reason for my question." He let a page of the paper fall back and the implication of his words sink in.

Sargesson made a noise in his throat and closed his eyes. He felt suddenly tired and wished that someone would call him, that he could end the interview in some way.

"Of course there is another possibility" — Peyrouse's voice was casual — "that somebody could have killed Kemp and driven the car, wearing Kemp's clothes over the rubber suit."

"Why should anyone do that?"

"Someone perhaps with a knowledge of forensic medicine, who knows what modern methods of analysis . . ."

"Well that's something I've never . . ." Sargesson stopped abruptly. Then he went on, "I don't think anyone around this hospital has had that kind of training." The silence descended again and Sargesson wished he hadn't spoken.

"Then we have two hypotheses, but alas, we have no body and no rubber suit. Do you follow me, Doctor? He could have been killed here, he could have called on someone that last morning, they could have killed him, driven to Finisterre, and put the body in the current. If he had called on someone."

Sargesson never knew what sixth sense made him

say it, but his voice was quite calm. "As a matter of fact, Inspector, he called on me."

They waited again. The battered face was expressionless. Then Peyrouse said, "I knew that already, Doctor. I showed photographs of the car to the neighbors and one of them remembered seeing it there early on the morning of Kemp's departure. I knew that already, but I'm glad that you have told me."

"And do you think I murdered him?"

Peyrouse hesitated. "In our work we listen continually to evidence. . . . Every day is made up of it. One develops an instinct for truth . . . for people." He smiled. "I do not think you could kill someone, Doctor." He stood up. "Besides, my witness saw Doctor Kemp drive away alone."

With a sudden movement Peyrouse bent forward and picked up the spool of lavender thread. "Don't tell me that you sew up your patients with *this.*"

"No, I was taking it home. Some mending . . ."

"It is a very exotic color for a man."

And Sargesson said, conscious that he was speaking a little wildly, "It's for a shirt . . . a sport shirt."

"Ah . . . *le sport.*"

In another period of silence Sargesson's explanation seemed to disintegrate between them. He said, "You said you were going to Grenoble. I thought you'd gone."

"*Ah, oui.* Soon I must leave." But Peyrouse's voice held all the false optimism of some character out of Chekhov. "It is my way ahead . . . through Grenoble. A course of instruction and then another post. New cases . . . it is not unlike the life of a *docteur,* would you say?

Terminal cases die, a new patient comes to the bed and you begin again. . . ."

"But you said investigations never die."

"That is so. That is why I'm spending my time on this . . . this conundrum here." He flicked the dossier with his small pale finger. "Conundrum? That is the correct English word?"

"I guess it's one you could use. It's certainly a puzzle."

Peyrouse watched him steadily for a moment and smiled. Sargesson relaxed. Then Peyrouse said, "Do you treat mental patients?"

"We treat some cases here in the hospital, neurosis rather than psychosis, but it isn't in my department, of course." Sargesson glanced at his watch. "Doctor Weiss is a part-time consultant here . . . if you'd like to speak with him."

"*Ah, non.* I was just curious. Why do you have a *camisole de force*? A straitjacket? Is that the word?"

Sargesson said, "A straitjacket?"

"A straitjacket." Peyrouse repeated it again slowly as if giving Sargesson more time to consider his answer. The seconds ticked away.

Sargesson muttered, "I don't quite follow you. . . ."

"Forgive me, Doctor, my curiosity again. I was examining the other room to occupy my time while I was waiting for you, and I saw this object rolled up in your closet."

Sargesson shrugged. "I guess I got hold of it sometime in case we had need of it here."

"When would that be?"

"Hell, I can't remember...."

"Such things come from a store?"

After a short silence Sargesson said, "The Dispensary handles most things we need. They send out for anything they haven't got."

"And you sign a bill when you obtain something?"

Sargesson let his breath go. "That's right." He looked at his watch again and stroked his head briefly. He was conscious of sweat on his hairline. He laughed mechanically. "You sound like you're still investigating me, Inspector."

"You were his ... his *confrère*. What you say is of interest because it might reflect some knowledge of him."

"Well, I couldn't really have killed him anyway ... my Hippocratic oath."

Peyrouse smiled. "Doctor Crippen swore a similar oath, one presumes. Come," he added quickly, "I'm making a joke."

Sargesson laughed mechanically again. He stood up. Peyrouse picked up his dossier. There was a government coat-of-arms on the cover and some title scrawled on the corner, but Sargesson couldn't read what it was. Peyrouse said, "I have enjoyed talking to you." And he added obscurely, "You have helped to flavor my mind about this case."

Sargesson opened the door for him and with his heart sinking waited for the coda question that always came when his guard was dropping. He stood in the waiting room with his hands spread at his side, unwilling to open the door until it was over. But today Peyrouse kept on going and opened the outer door himself. He said, "You'll be glad when I go to Grenoble. Then you too will have peace."

"Well . . ."

"Do not deny it, Doctor." He put out a small hand in front of him, in the way he had, and Sargesson shook it. Turning away, Peyrouse said, "You have met Mrs. Kemp, I believe."

Sargesson nodded. "She came to see me here."

"Ah, oui." He still held the door open. "A melancholy time for her. She is a woman in need of consolation." And he added dryly, "One hopes you were able to console her." He went on through the door without looking back. Sargesson watched him go off down the sterile corridor with the file hugged tight under one arm.

He closed the door slowly, pushed up the stud that operated the lock and went back to his desk. The case was not closed, as he had believed. The verdict of presumed death by drowning had not stopped the investigation. Of course he had known all along that police forensic experts would examine the car, which was why he'd worn Kemp's clothes over the diving suit when he drove it across France. But all Peyrouse would ever have was a hypothesis because he would never have the body, and the scuba suit had been consumed in the hospital boilers and its ashes were long scattered to the far winds on some city dump.

A light was glowing on his desk panel and he picked

up the phone. Josh said, "Got a couple of minutes, Sarge?"

He hesitated, then said finally, "Not right now, Josh. Maybe later. Can I call you back?"

"Maybe we could have a drink at the Pheasant before you take off into the bush."

"Well, that I can't do either. I have a call to make on the way home. Why don't I call you tomorrow?"

Josh said, "Okay then," in a tired voice, which indicated he wasn't happy.

Twice on the way home he pulled off his regular
route and turned into a side road.

But nobody followed him, and after waiting a couple
of minutes or so he drove on again. He had to admit
that Peyrouse had left him feeling a bit jumpy.
Peyrouse had that way with him. Somehow just picking
up a harmless spool of colored thread he'd managed to
give the impression that it was a bloodstained dagger,
so right away he was trying to explain things that had
no need of an explanation.

It was market day in Beaulieu and he was just in
time for most of the stores. After he'd shopped and got
into the car he drove up to the high Corniche and
followed it a way before dropping down at Eze.
Nietzsche had walked beneath the castle there, he remembered, down to the beach and back. He would have
to start doing more walking himself. Pretty soon he
wouldn't be driving this way anymore, because after
the interview with Peyrouse that afternoon and after

talking to Josh on the phone, he had sat at his desk hatching a momentous decision.

He'd retire in the spring.

He had computed his pension and checked investment schedules, and there was no doubt that he was pretty well heeled, more than enough for the humble needs of himself and Kemp. Not only that, with more time on his hands and a bit of money, he would be able to improve the setup considerably. It was still light when he put the car away in the barn and afterward he walked around the house, carefully keeping in the shadow of the trees. The aspens had lost some of their leaves now, and the seed pods of wild clematis hung from their branches like party decorations.

Inside, he lay down on the chaise with his cocktail, thinking again about retirement. He wouldn't tell Kemp, of course, not yet, in case anything went wrong. He was playing Noel Coward tonight, the music from *Bitter Sweet,* but it wasn't one of his favorites. It lacked the edge of the American musicals. It was too slushy, too sentimental.

In the end when he rose to freshen his drink he changed the record for an old Cole Porter. Then he lay back swinging the locket with one hand and thinking about the retirement idea again. He'd get the garden into shape, that would be one of the first things, and then maybe he'd do a bit of part-time consultancy at the hospital, just to keep his hand in.

Then again he might be able to find something else for Kemp to do, within the confines of his cell, of course. Again, for no reason he thought of Jeremy

Stuart, who seemed to have some pretty unusual inter-
ests. He and Kemp might even work out some project
together. Thinking of Kemp reminded him that it was
just about time he went down there. He tucked the
locket away in his top pocket, where he had taken to
carrying it lately. Whenever he was thinking about a
problem he tended to play with it as he might have
played with worry beads. He left his drink and went
through to the kitchen to get things together.

When he looked through the peephole Kemp was
lying on the bed in what had lately become his characteristic position, with his back to the hole and one hand
raised by his shoulder. Sargesson spun the handle that
opened the service door. He'd hardly crossed to the
work table before he heard Kemp at the grille.

"Have you got it?"

He put the paper bag down before he turned. "Got
what?"

"The thread. Did you remember the thread?"

Sargesson sighed. "Yes, I remembered the thread."
He went out again for the two buckets he'd left at the
head of the stairs.

As he came back, Kemp said, "Where is it?"

"Just wait a moment . . ." He went back to close the
door at the head of the staircase and then he came
down again, taking the spool of thread from his pocket.
He had tucked a needle through it.

He was laying it on the table when Kemp said, "Let
me *see* it."

"Oh Jesus . . ." But he held it up all the same. "And a
needle."

"It's too dark."

"It's the only shade of lavender they had. And anyway, it looks fine to me." He moved over to the bicycle and held it against Kiki's dress. "You really can't bitch about that, Kemp. It's identical."

"It's too dark," said Kemp stubbornly.

Sargesson threw it down on the table and went out. He closed the service door and opened the door from the cell. He stayed watching through the grille as Kemp blundered through and picked up the thread and held it to the light. Then Kemp spun away and came down toward him and the next moment a towel was flung up, blocking out the view.

Sargesson moved away quietly and picked up the periscope. He removed the plug and pushed it through, reversing the normal position of the mirror so that it reflected the open cell door to the utility room. Through it he could see Kemp standing face-to-face with Kiki. He was drawing the dress from her body as tenderly as if she had been a flesh and blood lover. Then he picked Kiki up and moved her away, out of Sargesson's line of vision. Sargesson waited another couple of minutes but there was no sign of Kemp, so he put away the periscope and went silently upstairs.

He carried the last drink in the shaker into the kitchen and started filling the pan with a mixed grill. He stood over it while it cooked, turning the bloodless pieces which had come foil-wrapped from the supermarket. He frowned. He knew that pretty soon something would have to be done about Kiki. The whole idea of introducing Kiki had been to help solve a sexual problem, but Kemp was getting obsessive, behaving in a way that was pretty damn stupid. Sargesson shook the pan irritably, moving the pieces around. It was unhealthy as well, lavishing attention on Kiki that wasn't actually sexual.

He remembered that a couple of months back Kemp had always been waiting to talk to *him* in the evening, to hear about *his* day on the wards. Now he wasn't interested anymore. Three or four nights a week Kemp was spending with her, blotting out the world with a towel. Sargesson broke an egg into the corner of the pan, the one egg he allowed himself a week, and watched it spread around and bubble. Something would have to be done, and it could only mean getting rid of the bitch. There was a limit to anthropomorphism.

When he went down later, the towel had gone and so had Kemp. Looking into the utility room he could see Kiki astride the exercise bicycle. Kemp hadn't shortened her skirt all that much. It was still just below the knee. He pushed through the periscope, and when he looked at Kemp he was lying down again and the raised hand was moving gently to and fro in time to the music he was listening to. It was boring, polyphonic music, Bach he guessed, or somebody like that. He reached sideways and spun the top wheel, locking the cell door.

When he opened up the utility room and went in, Kemp had laid out everything neatly, as usual. He took the buckets up first and then came back for the kitchen waste. Before he left he made the usual check to make sure Kemp had taken nothing into his cell except his night bucket and the food tray for the following day.

He went over to the grille. "Kemp?" He had to call twice before Kemp heard him over the music. And when Kemp came he said, "Where's the thread?"

"I don't know . . . on the table." Sargesson went to look again and found it behind the coffeepot. As he came back, Kemp said, "I might need it again."

"I'm sorry. You know the rules, only bare essentials."

"How would you rate a bunch of flowers?"

"We've discussed that before, and you know my opinion. It takes me all my time to keep up with ordinary supplies."

"This is something special, Sarge . . . it's Kiki's birthday tomorrow."

"Oh, don't be so fucking crazy."

"I *mean* it." Sargesson started to move, going back to the passage. "Sarge, please . . . I swear I'll never ask you for anything extra again."

Sargesson turned and came close to the grille. He said, "Kemp, you really are starting to act a little crazy over that woman. And I reckon we're going to have to do something about it."

"What, Sarge?"

He could see Kemp close against the grille, his face segmented by it. Then Kemp had spun away and the dreary music stopped abruptly. As he went out into the passage, Kemp said in a deadly kind of way, "What do you mean by that?"

Sargesson closed the utility room door and started spinning the wheel. He could still hear Kemp's faintly anxious voice. "You wouldn't take her away, Sarge. You'd never do that."

Then as the bolts went home and Sargesson moved

off, Kemp's voice rose to a shout. "You can't fucking well *do* that! It would be inhuman. Inhuman, do you hear? After all it was your idea in the first place, Sarge. Sarge, come back here! Sarge, you've got to talk to me. . . ." At the top of the stairs Sargesson closed the soundproof door, shutting off the faint voice.

Kemp jogged for half an hour and then sang for a while, about ten minutes, because he'd found that unless he kept using his voice he somehow lost the tension in his vocal cords and became hoarse very quickly. After an hour there was still no sign of the periscope.

He jogged down to the grille and looked through at Kiki. "You're looking swell," he whispered. "You really deserve those goddam flowers."

ON FRIDAYS HE OFTEN DROVE OUT TO ST. LAURENT AT THE river mouth west of Nice, where they had a market. He had gone that day to buy fresh tuna fish and a few of the other things he needed, like a block of Cantal cheese, which Kemp used a lot in his cooking and dressings. He hesitated over some of the other cheeses, wondering whether he would surprise Kemp with some goat cheese or one of the Norman blues. Maybe tomorrow. He moved away, passing a stall hung with harness equipment.

Once, in the beginning, when he was afraid Kemp was going to be violent and uncontrollable, he had considered buying chain there, and a couple of bolt shackles. There was one with a staple big enough to hold a man's ankle, and it would have been a simple matter to flatten the threaded end of the bolt with a hammer. He walked on, putting the thought, which was now uncomfortable, out of his mind. At the end of the market, on the ramp that ran up to the parking lot, there was a little old lady sitting among cans of fresh flowers. Sargesson hadn't intended buying any; in fact he still wasn't sure that Kemp wasn't kidding him just a little. But seeing them there, he stopped and bought a bunch of mimosa. And then, because the irises were only a franc each, he bought half a dozen of them as well. He walked on up the ramp toward the car.

Josh was leaning against it.

Sargesson walked on steadily without checking, but his mind had raced ahead deciding the best plan of action. He'd go straight to the trunk and unlock it and drop the stuff in. Not that there was anything strange about his basket except suddenly there seemed to be a hell of a lot of flowers.

As he came up Josh said, "Hi, Sarge. I thought I recognized your plates. Can I ride home with you?"

"Surely. What are you doing here anyway?"

"I came out on the bus to Cap Trois Mille and I had a little time to kill. Here, let me help you. . . ."

"It's okay."

But Josh came to hold the flowers and the basket while he fiddled with the lock of the trunk. Josh sniffed the mimosa before dropping it in. "I love that stuff," he said noncommittally.

They drove in silence out onto the freeway, running eventually into the Promenade des Anglais. Then Josh said, "As a matter of fact that was pretty well met, because I really do have something to say to you. You promised to call me back this morning."

"Sorry, Josh, but I had a lot going on."

"This is important, but it needn't take long. Why don't we pull off somewhere quiet right now?"

Sargesson said, "Right." He glanced at his watch. "But I'm telling you I've got rounds at a quarter after three."

"That's long enough."

Sargesson drove on, leaving the main road and sticking to the coast. He went by the hospital and arrived at a scattering of cars parked on a scenic pull-off overlooking Cap Ferrat.

The bay was full of yachts, and a two-hundred-meter power cruiser was moored just below them. There was a party going on, and tenders arrived continuously from the quay at Villefranche. It was mostly below decks, but a man stood at the stern with a half-dressed girl hanging on his neck. She was so still that she could have passed out.

Josh was saying, "I want a clear run, Sarge. I have something I have to get off my chest." Sargesson didn't answer and Josh went on, "I'm getting very worried about you because lately you've been showing symptoms."

"Oh, come off it, Josh. . . ."

"Listen," Josh said harshly, "because I am going to say it. Your condition isn't original, Sarge. You are right out of the textbook. An only son, raised by an adoring mother who died early. Next, a wife who only stays two years and then runs out. Then, fourteen years with Marion, and she dies. Women have always failed you."

He waited a moment looking at Sarge, but Sarge was staring down at the yacht with an expressionless face. A couple of American naval officers were going up the gangplank from the tender; maybe that unit of the

Sixth Fleet had finally gotten here. And at the stern the man and the half-dressed girl were moving in a slow semicircle doing some kind of drunken dance.

"After Marion died you made the classic responses and in the end, somewhere around three months ago I guess, you reattached yourself. That's the way it goes. Only because of *your* case history, with you it's different. Because of your record of imagined betrayal you are not ready to trust the world again. So whoever you've got out there at Bellegarde you're keeping to yourself. You don't want to share her with your friends or anyone else. Now I don't know who you've got hidden away there, but I do know you're pretty crazy about her. I'm not thinking of the flowers back there; I'm thinking of the fact you're so wrapped up in that woman she's taking all your devotion. There isn't even enough left over for your work. That's the word that's going around. Tom Hurst wants to put you on two months' leave of absence to see if you can straighten yourself out, but he agreed to let me talk to you first."

Josh's voice rambled on. Sargesson was motionless in his seat. At the beginning he had listened with the objectivity of a stranger, as if he and Josh had been talking across some patient in a bed, but as the ridiculous implication of what Josh was saying became clear, he felt a rush of feeling that was a compound of anger, shock, and disgust. It was a load of shit to say he had attached himself to Kemp. It was a typical headshrinker's screwed-up diagnosis.

On the yacht below, more people had moved up to group under the deck awnings, and Sargesson noticed some of them were in evening dress. Maybe the party had been going on all night.

Christ, the only reason Kemp was *there* was because he was a murderer. He felt a terrible need to be free, to be less constricted, and he opened the car door suddenly and got out. But Josh opened *his* door and stepped out and went on talking to him across the roof.

"I just had to speak up, Sarge, the same way you'd speak to a friend who showed obvious signs of hypertension or liver damage or whatever. But these obsessive conditions are sometimes easy to treat and they yield to psychotherapy in a lot of cases."

Sargesson walked away toward the parapet. One of the hands spread at his side was shaking uncontrollably. He tried to shut out Josh's voice, to push the crazy thing away. He concentrated on the yacht below. The half-dressed girl was now stepping out of her pants and bra before hanging herself back on the man, quite naked. None of the other guests seemed to be taking any notice, so Sargesson guessed that maybe he was the host.

"Sarge?" Josh came up behind him. "I must explain it to you, Sarge . . . your antisocial posture can end up in a way that could be dangerous. One prognosis leads to what Rudi Meyer and the German School call a *Nachtmarsch*. A night march simply means a state of mind where you develop patterns of behavior which run parallel with your normal life but are in fact upside down, like reflections. The paradox becomes the norm. It's a state of mind that can be triggered off by grief or deprivation — anything like that. And it all seems very logical to the patient. Even an ethic can be reversed. . . . Doctor Jekyll and Mr. Hyde is a kind of ludicrous extreme of a night march."

Sargesson turned around. "Okay, you've had your say. . . . Let's go!"

They drove back without speaking. Sargesson had to make a conscious effort not to speak, not to tell Josh what a load of shit he'd been talking. At the hospital gates Josh said, "You can put me down here."

"I'm going to the hospital."

Josh got out and leaned back in with a grim smile, the smile of a man who was hurt. "I have to go back and pick up my car at St. Laurent," he said in a grating voice. "So long, Sarge."

He limped away through the traffic to the taxi stand on the other side.

Sargesson walked with the assistant head nurse through a ward inspection that was largely routine.

When it was over he had tea in the Staff Room and then changed and went down to his car again. He drove back through Nice to Caucade. It was cold in the cemetery, although the sun was bright. Somewhere beyond Marion's grave, figures in black were grouped around another burial scene. The liturgical drone of the priest's voice just reached him.

He stood for about five minutes, remembering her in life, before he went back to the car.

WHEN HE RETURNED TO THE HOSPITAL THE PARKING LOT
was more crowded, and he had to park way down at the
end among the umbrella pines.

He got out with his medical case and locked up each
door in turn, checking the trunk as he walked around
the back. Then he set off with his sticklike walk
through the lane of cars. He had reached the stone-
paved path which led around to the front when he saw
Peyrouse sitting on the steps ahead of him. As he
stopped dead, Peyrouse stood up.

Sargesson got the same kind of shock as he always
did, as if he were facing an opponent, waiting for the
lunge. And now Peyrouse brought up one of his small
hands slowly, as if he were in fact raising a foil to the
tierce position.

In a slow voice that just reached him, Peyrouse said,
"The case is over, Doctor." Sargesson stayed where he
was, in a kind of paralysis. He was aware of the traffic
on the road below and a big jet on approach to Nice
airport only a few kilometers away.

Then Peyrouse said loudly, "I found Peter two hours ago. I've just come back from Bellegarde."

Sargesson spun awkwardly, stumbled on green moss or something, and then lumbered away with his topcoat flapping and the medical case swinging wildly. When he looked back over his shoulder he saw that Peyrouse was moving parallel to him. Peyrouse was shouting, but he couldn't hear the words. He half-walked, half-ran down the lane of cars and caught occasional glimpses of Peyrouse keeping pace with him in the next lane. He expected Peyrouse to blow a whistle, as would have happened in a movie. But all he heard was Peyrouse calling him without excitement. "Doctor?"

He couldn't reach his car, not the way he was going, he saw that now. He'd take another nearer the entrance.

Already gasping for breath, he sidestepped through two lanes and, looking back, saw that Peyrouse had slipped ahead of him and nearly caught up with him. He turned up the next lane toward the entrance, trying to move faster, but his legs somehow couldn't make it. Then ahead of him a car turned into the lane and stopped.

Ralph Bassadone's head came out of a side window. "What's up, Sarge?"

As he turned to go down between another couple of cars, he saw Ralph and Fran leaving the car with troubled faces. Then suddenly Peyrouse was there ahead of him between two cars, waiting.

He swung back toward the pines, but as he came clear of a minibus he saw Ralph already moving that

way. He turned again, slipped, hit the side of the minibus and slithered to his knees.

He heard Peyrouse from quite close say, "Please, Doctor. . . ," but he levered himself up. Then it was as if
he had some kind of aberration. Like a light-blinded
insect he just ran straight at the side of a car. He hit it
with a crunch and fell over in a heap. Lying curled on
his side, he saw the pens and thermometer case from
his top pocket spilled in the dust. He shifted awkwardly
as the others came up.

Ralph said rapidly. "What's going on, Sarge? Are you
okay?"

Fran said, "Sarge?"

Between their legs, about fifty meters away, he could
see two or three people who had just arrived staring at
him.

Still gasping for breath he looked wildly around and
then Peyrouse said calmly, "The *docteur* and I have
something to talk about. I'm afraid it is a matter of
some distress. . . ."

Ralph bent over him, taking him under the arms.
"Let's get you up."

While he stayed there against the car, his eyes locked
with Fran's. He managed a sad half-smile, and she
smiled back just as sadly. Ralph was tucking the pen-
cils and the thermometer back into his top pocket.
Peyrouse was holding the medical case as if he had
already taken formal possession of Sargesson.

He said, "The car of the *docteur* is over there," and
as they moved off, Fran took his arm.

"I'm really okay now," he said in a clear voice, but

she didn't let go. They went in a ragged group down to the car. He got the keys from his pocket, but Fran took them from him and opened the doors.

Peyrouse put the medical case on the rear seat. He said, "Thank you for your help."

"I'll stay with you," Fran said.

"No really . . . you've been great." And he managed to smile at Ralph. "Thanks a lot. See you. . . ." At last they turned uncertainly and walked away, up toward the main block.

"Sit down, Doctor."

Sargesson sat in the front passenger seat, which was nearest. Leaning in the door, Peyrouse said, "I know it was a shock for you, perhaps, but it was not necessary to behave like that."

He walked away around the car and got into the rear seat on the other side. Sargesson supposed he would now be charged, in the curiously stilted language that was always used, but Peyrouse said, "I know now that you were extremely devoted to your daughter." Sargesson waited with no particular emotion. It was almost as if it was happening to someone else. Then Peyrouse said, "I want to help you." Sargesson continued to wait without curiosity. "I know it is painful but the affair must be finished. He came to the Gendarmerie this morning . . . a priest had persuaded him to talk to me."

Sargesson failed to comprehend what the Inspector was saying. *"Who* came? . . ."

"Peter. Pierre Boutin, the brother of your daughter's friend. He was the boy at the funeral. Possibly you may remember him."

Sargesson whispered, "But his name's Pierre. . . ."

"Your daughter always called him Peter. They were, it seems, not only in love but lovers. And when she became *enceinte* he was the one who found the old abortionist. He is already in prison, by the way, for another crime. I knew you would want to know immediately, so when you were not here I drove to Bellegarde to inform you." His voice rambled on but Sargesson heard it only as a counterpoint to his own thoughts. "Mother of God," his inner voice was saying. "What have I done!" He remembered the boy's pale triangular face at the funeral. And of course it was the boy who had left the roses at her grave that time.

What had happened to him, all those months ago when Marion died! What had he done! He let his head fall back on the headrest. But it couldn't have been anyone else but Kemp . . . the name Peter, the diary, Kemp's address there, Kemp's reputation as a womanizer, and finally his confession. He rolled his head blindly on the rest.

"Doctor?"

"Are you sure about the boy?" he whispered. "Is it certain?"

"*Ah, oui.* But I can see that it pains you to talk about it . . . to find out after all these months. Would you like me to make arrangements to have you taken home, Doctor?"

"No, no. I'll be fine in a minute."

"*Ah, bon.*" Peyrouse sighed. "The boy came just in time. This morning before I saw him they had told me that at last I am to go to Grenoble. I take the *rapide* tonight." The car door opened and closed. Peyrouse's footsteps crunched around to where he was sitting. The door beside him opened. He saw Peyrouse's creased face, calm against the blue sky.

"But I wanted to tell you before I went," Peyrouse said, "because I know how much the matter has disturbed you." He waited. The long habitual silence passed. Away on the path a woman laughed and a car door slammed.

Then Peyrouse said, "I wanted to tell you so that your mind can now be at rest."

Sargesson waited.

A car drew away, the one with the laughing woman maybe. Two more cars arrived, one parked just below him. Nobody got out. Sargesson moved at last, levering his body across into the driver's seat. He backed out, pulled slowly away, braked gently at the white line to the boulevard. He pushed up the indicator stick to show he was turning left. Then he drove on in the same precise manner, as if he were following the catechism of a driving school. The instructor might have been sitting beside him.

On the lower Corniche he kept to the slow lane where there was one. Once a car pulled out and overtook him, a beat-up old Citroën, and it took a place just ahead of him. There was a girl kneeling in the back seat with her chin on her arms, staring back down the road. Her eyes were unregistered by some intensity of thought, and she looked just about Marion's age. His lips moved and he said, "Marion," quite loudly, surprising himself. He had done it all for Marion . . . something that had had to be done.

At Eze-sur-Mer he dropped from the Citroën and took the road up to the Moyenne Corniche. He continued to glance regularly in the rearview mirror and use his indicator meticulously. In the brilliance of the day the white stone of the Corniche was blinding. And then suddenly he saw the viaduct and a moment later he was driving up through the development and stopping in front of the iron gates.

He put the car in the barn as usual and carried the groceries into the house, the flowers on top of the paper bag nodding in his face. He laid them on the kitchen table and then, still moving mechanically, he went through into the living room to mix himself a drink in the shaker. The phone on the landing had started to tinkle, but he ignored it and after a while it stopped. He was in a limbo that had become familiar with experience, that had begun with his mother's death. Twice since, the central core of his life had been removed. It was like submitting to endless operations.

He left the olive floating in the glass and went back to the kitchen to start the ritual of buckets and groceries. He wanted time to recover from the shocks of the afternoon, to consider. He went down to the cellar and pushed the periscope through the hole. Kemp was asleep in his familiar position. In the ellipsoidal reflection of the small mirror he had the huddled look of a fetus in the womb. Sargesson opened the service door and went in. He heard Kemp yawning and stirring in the room beyond and he dropped the flowers on the table and hurried out before Kemp could get to the grille.

As he closed the service door and opened the cell door for Kemp he heard Kemp call, "Sarge?"

He didn't answer. As he walked away Kemp called again. "What's the bloody rush! Hey, Sarge!"

He went back to the kitchen and hesitated over the food in the freezer. In the end he decided to have cold tuna fish and salad. He washed the salad greens and dressed them in a glass bowl with oil and vinegar and a squirt from the garlic press. Then he went back to taste his drink and put on some music. He chose the selections from *Top Hat*, which he hadn't played in a long time. Sitting down with the drink, he tried to shut out the world. But tonight the music and the cocktail had no effect. His mind revolved in panic.

He could explain it all to Kemp, of course, and see what Kemp would do. Maybe Kemp would trade eternal silence for his freedom. Nobody would ever know. All that had happened was that Kemp had disappeared for several months, and then turned up again. But of course Kemp would never keep the bargain.

He emptied the shaker into the glass and swallowed half of the drink. He suddenly realized, with dreadful clarity, that he need do nothing at all. Things could just go on the way they were. From way back at college he remembered the words of some old British historian, who had written that the true measure of a man's character was what he would do if he knew he would never be found out. Sargesson realized that, preeminently, he was subject to that measure now. He walked the room with his hand out stiffly at his side.

Then in one brief moment he broke out of the prism of thought and realized what he'd been considering. He had been about to compound a terrible immorality. There was only one thing to do, and that was to go down and tell Kemp. He would tell Kemp in his cell; he wouldn't release him until they had talked about it. Kemp might be quite irrationally violent. He would tell Kemp the way he had told him everything else, through the grille, with its comforting illusion of a confessional.

He swallowed his drink, and when he put the glass down it rattled briefly. He walked out slowly and went down to the cellar and picked up the periscope. When he looked through Kemp was back in his usual position lying on the bed and he must have heard Sargesson because he waved a hand vaguely. Sargesson leaned sideways to close the cell door. Then he put down the periscope and opened the door to the utility room. As he went in Kemp suddenly called his name from behind.

He had half-turned, confused, when Kemp's naked body seemed to explode toward him and Kemp's head hit him in the side of the chest.

He staggered sideways as Kemp's weight went past him, and then he fell across the frame of the exercise bicycle.

Looking up, he saw Kemp braced against the other wall and he shook himself clear of the frame. "Kemp . . ." But even as he spoke the first heavy drops of blood hit the floor in front of him as his nose started up.

Then Kemp hit him again with alternate chops and punches. He could see Kemp's face, strained and fanatical, and once when it was close to his shoulder he smelled Kemp's hot breath like that of an animal. Then with sudden strength in his long skinny arms, he pushed Kemp away as hard as he could.

There was an intense pain in the region of his clavicle where one of Kemp's blows had fallen, and now blood was streaming down his front. Kemp had gone back onto the table and it had tipped over. He was kneeling in a mess of groceries and flowers.

"Stop, Kemp, please . . . you have to let me . . ." Sargesson flinched as a can of soup just missed his face and a moment later Kemp was grappling with him again. The force of Kemp's rush carried them both backward in a series of jerks through the door and into the passage. As his back met the far wall, Sargesson's knee came up lmost by accident but he felt it meet the softness of flesh and cartilage and the next moment Kemp had fallen on his hands and knees.

He reached down instinctively to pull Kemp up, but Kemp's naked body was slippery with blood and more was falling on it in a steady stream.

"Please, Kemp . . ."

As Kemp, still breathless, crawled toward the wall to pull himself up, Sargesson said loudly, "Kemp, I won't resist . . . I won't do anything. You can go now." But the face Kemp turned toward him was devoid of any human feeling, and Sargesson suddenly realized that Kemp wasn't going to stop until he'd killed him, that the long months of enforced confinement had fed Kemp's desperation to the point where Kemp would kill him to get free.

Somehow he had to get out of there.

Kemp had almost reached the wall when Sargesson moved, swinging a foot at his head. His shoe met bone and the centrifugal force of his long leg seemed to lift Kemp right up before he rolled over with his arms flopping wildly. He ended on his back with his head twisted sideways and his eyes closed. Sargesson took a step over him but his foot, when he put it down, was shot with excruciating pain. He cried out again, an effeminate sort of sound, more surprise than pain, and he waited, feeling his tear ducts fill. Then he limped heavily over Kemp's body to lean against the wall. Every gasping breath sent a spray of pink blood in front of him. He stayed leaning there nearly a minute while his breath count slowly subsided. Then he limped two or three painful steps toward the stairs. He stopped.

He couldn't leave Kemp like that. He came back and half-knelt on his good leg until he could get a hand under Kemp's shoulders. Then he straightened and moved, jerking Kemp's body about six inches at a time along the concrete floor. He limped on two paces, whimpering at the pain in his foot, until Kemp was in the middle of the passage and he had to stop.

It was then that he noticed something about Kemp's appearance that frightened him. He fumbled hurriedly for Kemp's wrist and felt nothing. His hands moved swiftly to grip Kemp's head, one crushing his nostrils, the other pulling down his jaw. He covered Kemp's mouth in the kiss of life and his breath went into Kemp's lungs in a series of long silent screams. On and on he went, trying to shock some sort of reaction out of Kemp's heart until his own body was collapsed over Kemp's. He didn't know how long he lay there gasping, only that suddenly he was aware of Kemp's face cold against his own. He stood up slowly without noticing the pain in his foot.

He said, "Kemp?" out loud.

Then, "It was an accident," he whispered, over and over again. "It was an accident."

Blood dripped from his chin onto Kemp's upturned face unnoticed. He turned away at last and started to staunch it with his handkerchief. His left side was beginning to hurt him just below the rib cage. He stood there for nearly five minutes, his panic abating gradually like the flow of blood from his nose.

"It was an accident." This time he said it loudly, with confidence. But how had it happened? How had Kemp gotten out? How?

He moved over to the open door of the utility room and one bloodstained hand spun the lock that opened the door of Kemp's cell. He walked through slowly, his other hand still holding the handkerchief to his nose. At the door of the cell he stopped in shock.

Kemp's figure still lay on the bed.

Sargesson moved at last, following the lavender thread across the cell. It went under the bed and came up the other end and back to Kiki's wrist. The wrist, he saw now, was tensioned by two rubber bands knotted together and tied to the bed frame, so that when Kemp had pulled and released the thread, the arm had waved just the way Kemp's used to. And Kemp had done a pretty good job on the rest of her. He'd shaved the visible half of her head and pasted his own dark hair clippings to the skull with a gray-looking mixture that was probably flour and water. And after he'd put his own clothes on her, he'd darkened her skin with something. It could have been gravy browning or the yeast extract that was Kemp's favorite spread.

For the last week Kemp had deliberately adopted that sleeping posture, with his back to the peephole and his right hand over his shoulder. He had always waved it when Sargesson called him. And the whole charade over the dress was only to get his hands on the length of thread. It had been worked out to the finest detail, and hanging the towel over the grill had given him privacy earlier to dress her up. Then when Sargesson had thought Kemp was lying on the bed waving his hand, and locked the door to his cell, Kemp had still been in the utility room pulling the thread and waiting for him to come in.

He realized now that Kemp had never gone around the bend over Kiki, that his whole sexual infatuation had been simulated. And that from the very first day he'd brought her back to the house, Kemp had started planning his escape.

She looked grotesque lying there, and, bending down, he started to undress her, gently unzipping Kemp's jeans and drawing them off. But it was too awkward with only one hand, and he left her there, half-clad, to go into the annex and pack his nose with tissue. Standing in front of the mirror, he remembered that he had checked the hair floating in the slop pail the night Kemp had cut his hair, but obviously Kemp had kept some of it back. And although he'd taken care to remove the spool of thread, Kemp must have unrolled some of it first. The rubber bands, he recognized, came from bunches of cress. But where had all the stuff been hidden? There *was* no hiding place. There was nothing that couldn't be instantly checked, as he checked now automatically. It had been his principal concern to make sure of that.

Then behind the door he saw Kiki's dress and under-clothes. Maybe Kemp had wrapped himself in them while he was waiting for Sargesson to come down. He picked them up carefully now and carried them through to the other cell. He knelt to unbutton Kemp's shirt and when he slipped it off her, he saw that Kemp had broken her articulated elbow joint to make the arm move more easily. He sat her up and then took up her panties and bra, smoothing the cold fabric with his hands. He pulled the panties up as far as her knees and then tilted her forward onto his shoulder. When he looked down her back he saw a lock of hair protruding from her anus. He laid her down again and his fingers quickly probed the rectum. There was another rubber band there and a paper clip besides the hair.

He had found Kemp's hiding place.

He had to confess to himself that he had never thought of looking there, and even if he had, a certain delicacy would have inhibited him. He had always thought of Kiki as Kemp's woman, and he hadn't wanted to know what Kemp was doing to her.

He fixed the big, open-tipped bra, moving her breasts until they were settled comfortably, before buttoning her into the lavender dress. Then he laid her down again so that only her own exotic profile showed to the room. Josh would have been pleased to know about Kiki. It was always great to have a diagnosis confirmed, and Josh would have been pleased to know that he was still on target with the betrayal theory and if you couldn't trust a plastic woman, who *could* you trust. Okay, Josh? Okay?

After he'd showered and changed he bound his foot

with tape, and repacked his nose with a twist of lint. Downstairs, he poured himself half a glass of malt whiskey and sat with it clasped in both hands. Kemp had tried to murder him, that's what he had to remember. Whatever he'd done, he'd done in self-defense. It was almost as if he were defending himself in court, until he realized abruptly that there would never be a court which could call him to account. Kemp was already officially dead. The coroner in Finisterre had pronounced that finding.

He stared at himself in the pier glass, rocking the tumbler of whiskey. There was no dilemma; he had protected himself against a murderer. There was no guilt, no night march, nothing that need disturb his conscience after tonight. Life could go on. He half raised the glass toward his reflection and drank a joyless toast. As the glass touched his lips he became aware of a distant drumming sound.

It was like hoofbeats somewhere in the night, as remote and apocalyptic as the cry of the owl had been up there on the hill. He stood and moved towards the french window. A pale hand was rapping at the pane. Peyrouse was standing there. Sargesson hesitated, feeling a kind of angry revulsion, before he opened the window.

"You said you were going, Peyrouse. You were catching the *rapide* tonight? . . ."

"I'm sorry, Doctor." Peyrouse stepped in with both his hands raised as if giving himself up to Sargesson's mercy. "This is not an official visit, I can assure you of that. Nobody knows I am here. . . . I walked up from the *métro*. The *rapide* does not leave until after mid-night, and I thought you would forgive me if I called on you one last time. As a friend."

"You're welcome, of course." Sargesson stepped away at last. "You're welcome. A *digestif*? I'm having one. A whiskey perhaps?"

"*Non merci.* I cannot be long. I must return to Nice before my train departs. But I wanted to speak to you first."

"What is it? What can you want now that the case is over?"

Peyrouse moved off around the room, preserving for almost a minute one of his silences. "From the beginning your innocence has weighed me down, Doctor." He hesitated. "And then today you suddenly behaved like someone suffering the tortures of the damned. It has troubled me continually since, that perhaps my enquiries have hurt you deeply. . . ."

Sargesson said, "I was upset. After you told me about the boy . . ."

"*Ah oui.*"

"You must have a *digestif*, Inspector . . . we may never meet again. Then I'll run you down to the station."

"Well, perhaps some whiskey . . ."

"I'll get the ice."

"*Non. . . .*"

"It's no trouble."

As Sargesson went down the passage to the kitchen, Peyrouse drifted after him. "I am in your debt, Doctor. You have been my host now several times."

Peyrouse turned, hesitated. "You have left a light on here," he said. He turned it off, stroking the switch in a gesture that was almost effeminate. He added, "I am always doing that myself."

But Peyrouse didn't move away. It was as if his brain had refused to accept the picture on his retina, the picture of a body in the cellar passage. He raised his arm stiffly and flicked the switch on again.

Sargesson watched helplessly as Peyrouse went quickly down the steps to kneel by Kemp's naked, blood-splashed body. He put down the ice bowl and started to follow but stopped in the doorway. He saw Peyrouse cross himself and then with the same effeminate brush of the hand as he had put out the light, he closed Kemp's eyelids.

Without turning he said, "Doctor Kemp looks younger than in his photographs." He stood up slowly, still without looking back at Sargesson. "You were waiting until I had gone, until the case was closed, before you killed him."

"No, Peyrouse . . . you are totally wrong." Sargesson almost stumbled in his haste to get down the steps.

He stopped as Peyrouse turned at last. In the glaring light the planes of Peyrouse's face were set implacably. "You were like a crooked gambler who had to know he had won before risking his stake."

"It was the other way round. *He* tried to kill me."

Peyrouse turned away. He moved through the door into the annex. "Have you any more bodies here?" His eyes swept the walls before he went on again into the cell where Kiki lay.

Following him, Sargesson said, "You have to listen to me, Peyrouse. . . . I can explain . . ."

"I'm sorry, Doctor." Peyrouse looked back at him, his face still a mask of stone. Then he bent to examine Kiki, fingering the lavender dress briefly. "Now I see why you required the thread." And after a pause he added grimly, "It is certainly unusual, *le sport* we were speaking of."

Then Peyrouse saw the locket. He thrust a hand into the deep cleft of her breasts and drew it out. In the same tone of inexorable irony he said, "And of course this was not for services rendered . . . you only wanted to get rid of it again."

From the doorway Sargesson said, "You must let me tell you everything, Peyrouse! Kemp murdered my daughter, he was trying to murder *me. . . .*"

Peyrouse's pitiless expression didn't change. Sargesson began to retreat slowly before it, shouting, "In the eyes of God I've done nothing wrong Peyrouse, nothing!" He turned abruptly and went through to the passage, closing the door.

As he spun the wheel lock, Peyrouse's face came up to the grille. "Now you have to listen to me." Sargesson's voice was desperately quite. "I'll begin at the beginning and I won't let you out until you've heard it all. Then you'll see that I'm innocent . . . that I had no choice. . . ."

THE CHILL OF AUTUMN WAS ALREADY IN THE AIR AS HE
left the *halles*. He was waiting to cross over to the Place
Charles de Gaulle when he heard her voice again as in a
remembered dream.

"Dr. Sargesson!"

She was moistening her lips when he turned. "Hilary
Osgood," she said. "I told my husband I'd seen you
recently and we both wondered whether you'd like to
come to dinner with us one evening. Now you're giving
up the hospital we thought . . ."

"I'm sorry, Mrs. Osgood, but I'm still pretty busy.
Maybe in a week or two . . ."

But she was staring down at his shopping basket and
the cartons of milk lying there. She said, "Another
yoghurt-making day?"

John Gill was born and brought up on an island in the South Pacific and now lives in Europe. Besides novels he has written plays for American and French television, where his work was nominated for the Grand Prix Albert Ollivier. He is married to an English painter and they have one daughter.